The Chrysalids

Long, long ago lived the Old People. No one knew just how long ago – perhaps two thousand years. We knew that they had many things we did not have now, like mines and high-powered engines and machines. But something terrible had happened to the Old People. It was worse than fire and earthquakes. We called it the Tribulation. Nearly all the Old People had died in the Tribulation.

Now, the world was divided into two parts. We lived in a land called Labrador. We had farms and fished in the sea. The sea lay round the north and east of Labrador. South of Labrador were the Badlands where the Tribulation had brought the Old People to their end. There was nothing but ruins. And if you went to the Badlands you died.

But in many ways Labrador was not safe either . . .

The BULLS-EYE series

General Editor   PATRICK NOBES

The Chrysalids

Adapted by Sue Gee
from *The Chrysalids*
by John Wyndham

Stanley Thornes (Publishers) Ltd

Original novel first published 1955
This adaptation first published 1975
Reprinted 1977, 1978, 1980, 1984, 1986, 1988

Reprinted 1990 by
Stanley Thornes (Publishers) Ltd
Ellenborough House
Wellington Street
CHELTENHAM GL50 1YD

Reprinted 1993

ISBN 0 7487 0279 2

Set in Intertype Baskerville

Printed and bound in Great Britain by
The Guernsey Press Co. Ltd., Guernsey,
Channel Islands

Contents

1 The City in My Dream

When I was quite young I sometimes dreamt about a city. It was odd, because the dream began before I even knew what a city was. But I could see this city, by a big bay, with boats on the water and houses all around. Sometimes I saw silver things flying in the sky. It was a pretty place.

Once I asked my sister, Mary, where the city was. She told me that there was no such place. She said that long ago there might have been a city like that, but not now. Then she told me not to talk about the dream to anyone.

Mary did not want me to talk about anything that might make people think I was different from them. Where we lived, people were always looking out for odd things. They even thought it was strange that I was left-handed. So I did not talk about my dream to anyone, and as I got older I did not have it so often.

And I never told anyone that I could talk to my cousin Rosalind without seeing her. I wasn't sure if talking like that *was* odd. After some time I thought perhaps I was just like everyone else. Until the day I met Sophie.

One day I had gone off by myself, as I often did. I went down a cart-track from our farm until I came to a high bank. This bank was very long, and ran all the way round the land, as far as you could see. I had often gone along the top of it, but I hadn't been down the other side. Somehow the land on the other side seemed strange, like another country. But today I played a game.

The rain had worn away some of the bank on the other

side and I could push myself down the path made by the rain. I did this twice, rushing down the bank and landing in the soft sand at the bottom. The third time I landed, a voice said 'Hello.'

2 I Meet Sophie

I looked around. At first I could not tell where the voice came from. Then I saw some bushes shaking. A face looked out at me from the bushes. It was a small face, brown from the sun, with curly, dark hair. It was the face of a girl.

'Hello,' I said.

The girl came slowly out of the bushes. She was shorter and younger than me. She wore brown jeans and a yellow shirt. On the shirt was a cross. All the women I knew had a cross on their clothes, but I stared at this girl because she was a stranger.

'What's your name?' I asked her.

'Sophie,' she told me. 'What's yours?'

I told her my name was David, and then I said, 'Where's your home?'

She waved her hand at the land beyond the bank. 'Over there,' she said. She looked at the path in the bank that the rain had worn away.

'Is it fun sliding down the bank?' she asked.

'Yes,' I told her. 'Come and try.'

For a moment she hung back. Then she ran up the bank and slid down very fast. When she reached the bottom she looked very pleased.

'I want to do it again,' she said.

The third time she slid down, she landed a few feet from

the usual place. I waited for her to get up, so that I could go next. She didn't move.

'Go on,' I said.

She tried to move, then she called up to me,

'I can't. It hurts.'

I slid down beside her.

'What's the matter?' I asked.

There were tears in her eyes.

'My foot is stuck,' she said.

Her left foot was under a pile of sand. I pushed the sand away. Her foot was stuck between two stones. I tried to move it, but I couldn't.

'Can't you get it out?' I asked.

She tried, her lips shut tight.

'It won't come.'

'I'll help pull,' I said.

'No, no! It hurts,' she cried.

I did not know what to do. I could see that Sophie was in pain.

'We must cut the laces. Then you can pull your foot out of the shoe,' I said.

'No!' she said quickly. 'No, I mustn't.'

I couldn't see why she didn't want to take her shoe off. If she kept it on she would be trapped.

'Oh, it is hurting so,' she said. She began to cry.

'You'll *have* to take your shoe off,' I told her.

'No,' she said again. 'I must never take it off.'

'If you don't take it off you will have to stay here. And if you stay I think you'll die,' I said.

At last she said I could cut the laces, but she looked very scared as I cut them. Then she said, 'Go away! You mustn't look.'

I walked away. Then I heard her crying again.

'I can't get the shoe off,' she said. 'If you take it off you mustn't ever tell anyone what you see. Never, *never*! Promise?' I promised.

She was very brave. When I did get the shoe off, her foot was very puffed up. Then I saw that she had six toes . . .

I pulled the shoe out of the gap in the rocks and gave it to her. But her foot was so puffed up that she couldn't wear it. She was still in great pain and she couldn't walk. I tried to carry her but she was too heavy.

Then she tried to crawl. She crawled until her knees began to bleed but then she had to stop. She showed me where her home was. I could see smoke from the chimney. Sophie crawled back to the bushes while I went to her home.

I knocked at the door. A tall woman opened it. She was very good-looking. She wore a brown dress and the big cross on the front was green, like her headscarf.

'Are you Sophie's mother?' I asked.

She frowned at me.

'What is it?' she said. She sounded worried.

I told her that Sophie had hurt her foot and was still in the woods.

'Oh!' she cried. 'Her foot! Where is she?'

I led her to the place where I had left Sophie. As she heard her mother's voice Sophie crawled out from the bushes. Her mother looked at Sophie's twisted foot and bleeding knees.

'Oh, my poor darling!' she said, holding and kissing her. Then she said: 'Has this boy seen your foot?'

'Yes,' Sophie told her. 'I'm sorry, Mummy. I tried hard, but I couldn't get my foot free by myself. It did hurt so.'

Her mother looked sad.

'Oh, well, it doesn't matter now,' she said. 'Up you get.'

Sophie climbed on to her mother's back and we all went back to the house.

3 The Secret

All my life I had listened to what my parents and other
grown-ups told me. I knew that there were laws, which told
you what people should look like. I knew that everyone was
supposed to have one body, two arms and two legs, four
fingers and a thumb on each hand. I knew that everyone
should have five toes. But I didn't think of any of this
while I watched Sophie's foot being bandaged. I looked
round the room where we were sitting. I saw that there
were no notices on the walls with laws written on them. At
home there were notices everywhere.

Sophie's mother seemed very kind. She was called Mrs
Wender. I felt happy with her. She was kinder than my own
mother. When Sophie's foot had been bandaged, her
mother took her upstairs. When Mrs Wender came back
she took my hand and looked at me very hard.

I could see her thoughts. I knew she was very worried,
and I tried to send my thoughts to her to say that everything
would be all right.

Mrs Wender nodded. She said in words:

'You're a good boy, David, and you helped Sophie very
much. Will you keep a secret for her? It is very important.'

'Yes,' I said, but I didn't know what the secret was.

'It's about Sophie's foot,' said Mrs Wender. 'No one else
has seen that she has six toes on each foot. You are the only
person who has seen her foot, except for her father and me.
You must never, ever, tell anyone. Do you promise?'

I could see her thoughts again. She was very frightened.

'If anyone ever found out the secret they'd be very
unkind to Sophie,' she said. 'Do you promise you'll keep
the secret?'

I did not think it mattered that Sophie had six toes. But

I could tell that Mrs Wender thought it was very important. So I promised to keep the secret.

We said goodbye, and Mrs Wender said that I could come and see Sophie again. But I must promise not to tell anyone where I was going.

I walked home slowly. As I walked, I thought for the first time about the laws. The laws said that anyone who was different from other people, in any way at all, was not human. And they said that anyone who was different was wicked, and that God hated them. I could not think that anyone would hate Sophie just because she had six toes. But I went home feeling very worried.

4   Norms and Mutants

When I reached home I waited until nobody was around. Then I crept across the farmyard and climbed through a window. I went up to my room. I wanted to think about what had happened. I knew that I would never be able to talk about Sophie to my family.

We lived in a big house called Waknuk, on a farm. All the land around our farm was called Waknuk too. But the country was called Labrador. Inside the house was a big kitchen. Our house was the biggest and best in Waknuk, and so was our kitchen. It had a very big fireplace, made of stone bricks. The floor was brick and stone, the walls were white, and there were tables and chairs, all very clean.

My father was a very important man in Waknuk. When he was sixteen he had given his first talk in church. At that time there were less than sixty families in Waknuk.

Now there were very many more. But my father still owned more land that anyone else, and he still talked in the church on Sundays.

My father was a very strict man, and he had strong beliefs about what was right. All over the house there were notices on the walls. I knew them by heart. They said *Blessed is the Norm* and *Look out for the Mutant.*

The Norm meant right and normal. Everyone who had the right number of eyes and ears and other parts of the body was a Norm. Everyone who was the right shape and not too tall or short was a Norm. A Mutant was someone who did not look like the Norm. You were a Mutant even if you only had a little thing that made you different from other people. These words were used for animals too, and even plants.

Another word used for things that were not normal was OFFENCE. So a Mutant was the same thing as an Offence. People thought that Offences were wicked. They though that if a child was not born a Norm, it meant that God was angry with the parents. So the child was killed. If animals were born with two heads or five legs, or anything else strange, they were killed as well.

My father was very strict about the laws. If he found an Offence on the farm he would get very angry. He would say prayers and ask God to forgive us for having an Offence on the farm. Then we would all get up early and go into the yard to watch my father kill the Offence. All Mutants and Offences were treated in this way.

If there were any plants in the fields which were Offences my father would pull them out and throw them away. Sometimes a whole field was an Offence. Then my father set the field on fire. My father was more strict about the Offences than anyone else we knew. Some people said he was too strict. But he always thought he was right.

Beyond Waknuk were other parts of the country of Labrador. First there was the Wild Country. There, only about half of anything – people, animals and plants – was a Norm. Beyond the Wild Country were the Fringes.

People lived in the Fringes. But these people were Mutants. Somehow, these Mutants had escaped being killed. They lived very hard lives and often they didn't have enough to eat. When they were hungry they would travel across the Wild Country to Waknuk to steal food. They would steal clothes and weapons as well. Sometimes they stole children. Often they came in small bands. At other times they came in big bands and did a lot of damage to the Waknuk farms.

All the children in Waknuk were afraid of the people from the Fringes. Our parents told us stories about people like Hairy Jack, who lived in the Fringes. They said Hairy Jack was like a monster, with a long tail. They said he ate children for supper.

Beyond the Fringes were the Badlands, where no one had ever been. There were many things to frighten us.

But usually we were quite happy. There was plenty of work on the farm, I had my cousin Rosalind to play with, and my Uncle Axel to talk to. Tonight, I did not come down from my room until supper-time. I didn't want anyone to see me. When I came down for supper, I saw the notice *Look out for the Mutant*. But I was too hungry to worry about that now.

5 If I Had Another Hand . . .

I went over to see Sophie once or twice a week after that. On the farm we had lessons only in the mornings. It was quite easy to get away later on. When I had gone, everyone thought that someone else had given me a job to do, so they stopped looking for me.

Sophie's ankle got better and she liked to show me the places she liked best near where she lived. And one day I showed her one of mine — the place where the great steam engine was kept. It was the only one for a hundred miles. We stood at the door of the shed where it was kept. We watched its wooden beams moving up and down with a very loud noise.

'My Uncle Axel says the Old People must have had much better engines than this,' I said.

Sophie said that her father thought that people talked a lot of nonsense about the Old People.

'But they were wonderful,' I said.

'Too wonderful to be true, my father says,' said Sophie.

I asked her if she thought that the Old People could fly.

She shook her head. 'If they could fly, we would be able to,' she said. 'Things can either fly or they can't, and we can't.' I wondered if I should tell her about my dream, and about the things in the sky that flew. But I decided not to. We set off for Sophie's home.

On the way we met Sophie's father. I had seen him several times and I liked him very much. But I wasn't sure if he thought I would keep the secret about Sophie's six toes. When I was older I understood why he was so worried that I knew the secret. If my father found out, Sophie would be in great danger. My father was very strict. He would call Sophie an Offence. And I've told you what he did with those! But something happened one day that made me see how important it was to keep the secret.

I had run a splinter in my hand. When I pulled it out, my hand bled a lot. When I went into the kitchen everyone was very busy. So I found a rag and tried to tie it on my finger. Then my mother saw me. She made me wash the finger and then she tied the rag on. She said, 'You would

15

have to do this when I'm busy.' I said I was sorry. Then I said :

'I could have tied it myself if I had another hand.'

Suddenly the whole room was silent. Everyone stared at me. My father looked at me. His face was very angry.

'What did you say, boy?' he asked.

I knew I had said something very wrong. I tried to say something, but I was very frightened.

'I – I s-said I couldn't tie the rag on by myself,' I told him.

'And you wished you had a third hand!' shouted my father.

'No, Father. I only said *if* I had another hand . . .'

'. . . you would be able to tie the rag. Wasn't that a wish?'

'I only meant *if*,' I said again. I saw that everyone was looking at my father. His face was grim.

'You – my own son – were asking the Devil to give you another hand!' he said.

'But I wasn't. I only . . .' I began.

'Be quiet, boy!' my father said. 'We all heard you. Don't lie now. You were saying that there is something wrong with the body God gave you. You said that the Norm was wrong. You know what the Norm is?'

I knew it was useless to try to explain again. I said :

'The Norm is the Image of God.'

'You *do* know. And yet you wanted to be a Mutant. What is a Mutant?' he asked.

'A thing hated by God and all men,' I said quietly.

'And *that* is what you wished to be!' he said. 'What have you to say?'

There was nothing I could say.

'Get down on your knees!' said my father. 'Kneel and pray.'

The others all knelt too. Then my father prayed for a long time. He asked God to forgive me and all the family for what I had said. Afterwards he sent me to my room and told me to pray again. Later that night he came and beat me, many times.

When he had gone, I lay in bed, wondering why it was so wrong that I had said 'If I had a third hand . . .' And I wondered what would have happened to me if I *had* been born with a third hand. Or an extra toe, like Sophie?

At last I fell asleep. I had a terrible dream. We were all standing in the yard, ready to kill a Mutant. And the Mutant was Sophie. My father moved towards her with a knife in his hand. Sophie ran round and round the yard, trying to hide her six toes, and crying for someone to help her. No one moved. My father took her and pulled her into the middle of the yard. Everyone sang a hymn. Then my father lifted the long blade of the knife . . . I woke up crying. If Sophie's parents had seen me then I think they would have known I would try not to give Sophie's secret away.

6 Talking in Think-Pictures

This was a time when a lot of things seemed to be happening. First I had met Sophie. Then, my Uncle Axel found out that I could talk to my cousin Rosalind without seeing her. Uncle Axel was my best friend on the farm.

I don't know why Rosalind and I had never told anyone that we could talk to each other like this. We called it talking in think-pictures. We had never told anyone, but we never thought it was an Offence to talk in think-pictures.

One day, I was sitting behind a hay-rick talking to Rosalind. I was talking aloud. Uncle Axel came up.

'And who are you talking to?' he asked, smiling. 'Fairies?'

I shook my head. He came and sat down beside me.

'Feeling lonely?' he asked.

'No,' I told him.

He frowned. 'Wouldn't it be more fun to talk to the other kids? Why talk just to yourself?' he said.

I wasn't sure if I should tell him that I wasn't talking to myself. Then, because he was my best friend among the grown-ups, I said: 'But I was talking to Rosalind.'

He looked at me hard. 'I can't see Rosalind,' he said.

'Oh, she isn't here. She's at home, in a little secret tree-house in the wood,' I said.

Uncle Axel couldn't understand what I meant at first. Then his face got very serious.

'Is this the truth you are telling me, David?' he asked. 'You really can talk to Rosalind without seeing her?'

'Yes, Uncle Axel, of course it's the truth,' I said.

'And you've never told anyone else about this?'

'No, never, it's a secret,' I told him.

He gave a sigh of relief. Then he said:

'David, I want you to make a promise. You must *keep* this secret. You must never tell anyone else what you have just told me – *never*. You must never do anything that would even let anyone else guess about it. When you're older you'll understand how important this is. Will you promise?'

I had never seen Uncle Axel be so serious. I made my promise and we shook hands on it. Then he said it would be best if I could forget all about it.

I thought about it, then shook my head.

'I don't think I could. It would be like trying to forget how to . . .' I began.

'Like trying to forget how to talk, or hear?' asked Uncle Axel.

'Rather like that, only different,' I said.

'Do you hear the words inside your head?' my uncle asked.

'Well, not exactly "hear" and not exactly "see". There are sort of shapes. If you say the words out loud it helps you to understand the shapes,' I said.

'But you don't *have* to use words?' he asked.

'Oh no,' I said.

Uncle Axel then made me promise never to talk aloud again as I had been when he found me. And he told me to tell Rosalind what he had said. Then he made me shake hands on the secret again and he went away.

I had not told Uncle Axel that there were others who could talk in the same way as Rosalind and I could. I did not even know their names, but they were there all right. We often talked to each other. That night I told them all, Rosalind as well, what Uncle Axel had said. Somehow, we all knew that he was right and that we must tell nobody about our secret way of talking. All the others promised not to tell anyone about it. When we made that promise to each other, we became a real group for the first time.

7 The Fringes People Attack

Very soon after we made that secret promise, the Fringes people tried to attack Waknuk. All over the country were small bands of our people. They had the job of warning everyone when they saw Fringes people coming. But the Fringes people knew how to hide. When there were a lot of them they attacked our small groups and killed the men.

Then they began to move through the country, stealing food and weapons. Soon they were only seven miles from our farm.

The farm became the place where our men got together to attack the Fringes people. For some days the farm was very busy as the men got ready for a battle. Our men had guns, and the Fringes people only had bows, knives or spears, and not many of those. Soon all the men were ready, and rode off on horses to battle. The women waved goodbye.

When they had gone, the farm was very quiet for a day. Then a man rode up very fast on a horse. He said that there had been a big battle. Some of the leaders of the Fringes people had been captured. The rest were running away as fast as they could.

In the afternoon a few of our men rode into the yard. With them were two of the captured Fringes people. I ran to look at them. I had heard so many stories about Fringes people. I thought I would see men with two heads, or with fur all over them. But these men looked the same as our men, though they were very dirty and wearing rags. One of them was a short man with fair hair. I looked at the second man and had a shock. He looked just like my father.

The man looked round and saw me. He looked at me very hard. I did not understand the look in his eyes ... He started to say something and then my father came out of the house. My father looked at the people in the yard. Then he, too, saw the man who looked like him. For a moment he looked hard. Then turned away and his face went grey.

I looked again at the man on the horse. He was sitting very still. As he looked at my father his face was full of hate. He looked like a wild animal. I never forgot that look of hate. My father looked very ill and went back into the house.

One of our men cut the rope on the Fringes man's arms. He got off his horse. Then I saw what was wrong with him. His legs were eighteen inches long too.

They were very thin and so were his arms. He looked like a huge spider. The man who had cut the rope gave the spider-man some beer and bread and cheese. He sat down and ate, and then he saw me again.

He made a sign for me to go to him. I slowly went up to him, but I kept away from his long spider-arms.

'What's your name, boy?' he asked.

'David,' I told him, 'David Strorm.'

He nodded. Then he said, 'Was the man at the door of the house your father? Is his name Joseph Strorm?'

'Yes,' I said.

He nodded again and looked round the farm.

'Is this place called Waknuk?' he asked.

'Yes,' I said again.

Then someone told me to go away. Soon all the men got on their horses again. They tied up the Fringes spider-man again and they all rode off. I watched them go. That was the first time I had seen a Fringes man. I had found it all very strange.

Later that night, I heard that both the captured Fringes men had escaped. I never heard my father talk about that day, and I was scared to ask him anything about it . . .

8 The Two Big Horses

The farm settled down after the battle and we all began to work again. But things were not quiet for long. Soon, my father had a row with my Uncle Angus, who was Rosalind's father. The family lived on the farm next to ours. My father and Uncle Angus were always having rows. My father thought Uncle Angus was a bad man because he was less strict than my father about Mutants and Offences.

This time they had a row because Uncle Angus had bought a pair of horses. My father had heard that the horses were very big and he went to see them. They were more than fifteen feet tall, and as soon as my father looked up at them he knew that they were *wrong*. No horses should be as big as that. He went to the inspector.

The inspector had the job of making sure that all Mutants and Offences were killed – plants, animals and people. But he thought that my father was too strict. When my father went to see him about Uncle Angus's horses, the inspector said that there was nothing he could do.

'The horses are a special kind. They are meant to be as big as that,' said the inspector.

'God never meant horses to be that big,' said my father.

'The Government says that these horses are not Offences,' said the inspector.

My father looked very angry.

'Then the Government is wrong,' he said. 'It is easy to see *why* some people would say these horses are not Offences. One of those beasts could do the work of two, maybe three, ordinary horses, and they need no more food than two ordinary horses do. People can make money out of beasts like these, but that doesn't mean the horses are all right.'

The two men looked at each other. They were both very angry. But there was nothing my father could do. He came home in a very bad mood. On the next Sunday he gave us all a long and angry talk. He said that my Uncle Angus was a wicked man and that the inspector and the Government were wicked too. The farm was not a happy place in those days and I was glad to go and see Sophie as often as possible.

Sophie could not go to school. If people there had found out that she had six toes they would say she was a Mutant and she would be in danger. So her parents tried to teach her at home. But they didn't have any books, so I tried to tell Sophie what I had learned about the world.

My books and my teachers had told me something about the history of our world, and about the land beyond Waknuk. All the land that was not Fringes or Badlands was called Labrador. It was a very cold land. Round most of Labrador was the sea, where people caught fish. I had never seen the sea – it was about three hundred miles north of Waknuk. In the south were the Fringes and then the Badlands, which would kill you.

Our history books only told us of the life that started about three hundred years ago. A very long time before that had been the time of the Old People. All we knew about them was that they had lived more than a thousand years ago. People now living thought that the Old People had once been very good, but had slowly grown wicked and forgotten the laws of God. Because they were wicked, God had sent them what we called Tribulation. The Tribulation had been something very bad, like an earthquake, which had killed the Old People. Our people thought that Mutants and Offences were still caused by the Tribulation. So it was very important now that everyone was a Norm and believed in God and tried to please him. If we killed all Mutants and Offences we would please God and slowly the world would become a good place. But if we did not please God, the Tribulation would come again and we would all be in danger.

I told Sophie a little of all this, but I did not talk much about killing Mutants. *I* never really thought she was a Mutant, but I knew that she was not really a Norm. I did not want to frighten her. And we had many other things to talk about.

9   Sophie's Secret is Found Out

Nobody at Waknuk seemed to worry about me if I was away. It was only if they saw me that they found jobs for me to do. That year had a good summer, very sunny, but with plenty of rain. Nearly all the plants which grew were Norms, and only a few sheep were Offences. Everyone was very busy working. They were very pleased that there were so few Offences on any of the farms nearby.

Only my Uncle Angus had trouble. The inspector made him burn a field of plants which were Offences. Everyone thought that his plants were Offences because he had bought the two big horses. They were glad that only he had been punished, and that nobody else had been.

When they were all working it was easy to get away. Sophie and I spent many days walking in the country. Sophie's parents had always told her not to talk to strangers. She was very good about this. The only grown-up she ever talked to was Corky. He looked after the steam engine. Sophie knew that all other grown-ups were dangerous. So we chose places where no one else went.

We had found a stream. I used to take off my shoes and go in the water, looking for little fish.

One day we took two nets that Sophie's mother had made, and a jar to put the fish in. I walked in the water and Sophie tried to catch fish from the bank. It was not very easy for her. She looked at me in the water.

Then she took off a shoe. She looked at her foot. She took off the other shoe, and walked into the water.

'Come over here,' I said. 'There are lots of fish here.'

She laughed and came over and we stayed in the water catching fish. Then we climbed onto a flat rock. The rock ran from the bank into the water. We let our feet dry in the sun.

Sophie looked at her feet. 'They're not really bad, are they?' she said.

'They are very pretty,' I said, and she was pleased.

A few days later we went there again. We left our jar and our shoes on the flat rock. When we caught any fish we went back to put them in the jar. We did not notice anything until suddenly a voice said :

'Hello, David!'

I looked up. Sophie stood very still behind me. A boy stood on the bank. He was just above the rock where our shoes and the jar were. I knew the boy. He was called Alan, and was the son of the blacksmith, the man who mended horses' shoes.

'Oh, hello, Alan,' I said.

I walked in the water to the rock and picked up Sophie's shoes. I threw them to her.

'Catch!' I said. She dropped one shoe into the water, but pulled it back.

'What are you doing?' asked Alan.

I had never liked Alan and I wished he would go away. I told him we were catching little fish. I came out of the water on to the rock.

Alan looked at Sophie. She was walking through the water to the bank further up the stream.

'Who is *she*?' asked Alan.

I put on my shoes and did not answer. Sophie had got out of the water and gone into the bushes on the bank.

'Who is she?' asked Alan again. Then he stopped talking and looked at the rock, beside me. I looked down. On the rock was Sophie's footprint. You could see the print of the six toes. Quickly I kicked over the jar. The water and the little fish poured over the footprint and washed it away. But I knew it was too late.

'Ho!' said Alan. I did not like the look in his eyes. 'Who is she?' Alan said again.

'She is a friend of mine,' I said.

'What is her name?' asked Alan.

I did not answer.

'I will soon find out anyway,' said Alan with a smile.

'It is nothing to do with you,' I told him.

He took no notice. He was looking along the bank to the place where Sophie had gone into the bushes.

I ran up the rock and jumped on him. We fought very hard. Alan was bigger than me and soon he began to win the fight. I fought back, but Alan sat on top of me, hitting me very hard. Then suddenly he stopped hitting me and shouted with pain. He fell on top of me. I pushed him off and sat up. Sophie was standing there with a large stone in her hand.

'I hit him,' she said. She sounded pleased and surprised. 'Do you think he is dead?' she asked.

She had hit Alan very hard. His face was white and he lay still. Blood ran down his face but he was breathing.

Sophie and I looked at Alan and then at each other. We were too afraid to help Alan. Sophie's mother had said, 'No one must ever know about Sophie's six toes. *No one*!' And Alan knew.

I took Sophie's hand. 'Come on,' I told her. We ran to her house.

10   Plans to Run Away

Sophie's father, John Wender, listened quietly while we told him what had happened at the stream. When we had finished the story he said:

'Are you quite sure that Alan saw the footprint?'

'Yes, he saw it,' I said. 'That is why he wanted to catch her.' Sophie's father nodded slowly.

'I see,' he said. I was surprised how calmly he said it. He looked at our faces. Then he turned to his wife.

'I am afraid it has come, my dear. This is it,' he said.

Mrs Wender started to cry. 'Oh Johnny . . .' she said to her husband. She looked very pale. Mr Wender put his arms round her and kissed her.

'I'm sorry, Martie, but we knew this would happen one day. How long will it take you to be ready?' he said.

'Not long,' said Mrs Wender.

She went to a cupboard and gave Sophie and me some food. 'Wash first, you dirty things,' she said. 'Then eat all of this.'

While I washed, I said to Mrs Wender, 'Why couldn't you cut off Sophie's extra toes when she was a baby?'

'There would have been marks, and people would have known why, David,' said Mrs Wender. 'Now hurry up and eat that supper.' She went out of the room.

When we were eating, Sophie said, 'We are going away. Mummy said we would have to go if anyone ever found out. We nearly went away when *you* saw my toes.'

'Do you mean, you must go right away? And never come back?' I asked.

'Yes, I think so,' said Sophie.

I did not want to eat any more. I looked at Sophie and felt very sad.

'Where will you go?' I asked.

'I don't know, but a long way,' Sophie said.

I watched the family packing their things. I was almost in tears. I knew nothing would ever be the same again after Sophie had gone. Mr Wender took some things outside to pack on the two horses, Spot and Sandy. I went out with him.

I watched him and then said, 'Why don't you use a cart?'

27

'Because with horses you can go where you like. You don't have to keep to the roads,' he said.

I watched him loading more things onto the horses. Then I said, 'Mr Wender, can I come too?'

He stopped what he was doing and looked at me. I looked back at him. Then, slowly and sadly, he shook his head. He took me back into the house.

Inside, he said to his wife, 'David wants to come with us.'

Mrs Wender sat down on a stool and held out her arms. I went to her. Looking over my head she said to Mr Wender:

'Oh, John. That awful father! I am afraid of what will happen to David.'

I could read Mrs Wender's thought before Mr Wender spoke again. I knew that she wanted me to go with them. But she knew that I must not go.

Mr Wender said to his wife, 'I am afraid for Sophie and you. If we were caught with David, people would say we had taken him away. And we would be punished even more. If we go away by ourselves we may escape. But if David comes too, everyone will be looking for him, and we will never escape.'

Mrs Wender said to me, 'You do understand why we can't take you, don't you, David? Your father would be so angry that we would have much less chance of getting Sophie away safely. Please be brave, David. You are Sophie's old friend, and you can help her by being brave.'

I knew before she spoke what she was going to say. When I had read her thoughts I knew that she was right. So I nodded, keeping back my tears. Then she held me close in a way my own mother never did.

The packing was finished just before dark. When the family was ready to go, Mr Wender took me away from the others.

He said that there was one more thing I could do for Sophie.

'Will you stay here tonight? Soon people will find Alan. He will tell them about Sophie. They will try to force the truth out of you. If you stay here they cannot talk to you. It will give us more time to get away,' he said.

I said I would stay and we shook hands. I felt stronger, knowing that Mr Wender trusted me.

When we went back to the others, Sophie held out her hand with something in it.

'This is for you, David,' she said. It was a piece of her hair, tied with yellow ribbon. I stared at it. Then Sophie put her arms round me and kissed me. Mr Wender picked her up and put her on one of the horses. Mrs Wender kissed me too.

'Goodbye, David dear,' she said. 'We will never forget all you have done.'

Then they left. I watched them ride off to the woods, waving goodbye.

It was a bad night. I was very frightened and the house seemed full of strange noises. I sat up for a long time watching the fire. Then at last I went to bed. The bed was in the main room and I lay watching the candles and the shadows on the walls. I listened to the strange noises. I thought about Sophie and knew I must stay in the house and keep my promise, even though I was afraid. At last I fell asleep, and when I woke up the sun was shining.

11 My Father Finds Out about Sophie

When I got home all the men were out in the fields working. But I saw the inspector's horse in the yard and thought my father would be in the house. I wanted to get to my room without anyone seeing me. I walked very quietly across the yard, but my sister Mary saw me from the kitchen window. She called:

'Come here at once. Everyone has been looking for you. Where have you been?' Before I could answer, she said, 'Father is very angry. You had better go to him quickly.'

My father and the inspector were in the front room. I went in. I had never seen my father look so angry.

'Come here!' he said when he saw me.

I went up to him slowly.

'Where have you been?' he asked me. 'You have been out all night. Where?'

He kept shouting questions at me, and grew more and more angry when I did not answer.

'Come on now – answer me! Who was this Mutant, this child you were with yesterday?' he shouted.

I still did not answer, but I felt sick with fright.

Then the inspector spoke quietly to me.

'Now, David,' he said, 'if you knew this child was a Mutant and you did not tell me, it is very, very serious. You could be sent to prison for it. Alan said that this child had six toes. Is that true?'

'No,' I said.

'He is lying,' said my father.

'I see,' said the inspector. 'Well, if she did not have six toes, it does not matter if we know who she is, does it?'

I did not answer that.

'I will deal with this. The boy is lying,' said my father. Then he said to me, 'Go to your room.'

I knew that my father was so angry that he would beat me even if I told him about Sophie. So I began to leave the room. My father followed, picking up a whip from the table.

'That is my whip,' said the inspector.

My father pretended he had not heard. The inspector stood up.

'I said that is *my* whip,' he said again. His voice was hard.

My father stopped and then angrily threw the whip back on the table. Then he followed me out of the room.

I had meant to keep my promise to Sophie and her parents. I did not want to tell my father the truth about Sophie's six toes. But he beat me so hard that I could not help telling him.

After he had gone, Mary came to my room. She cried when she saw my back. There were marks where my father had beaten me. She bandaged my back and gave me some soup. While she was there I did not cry, but when she had gone my tears ran on to my pillow. I felt very wrong because I had broken my promise. Feeling wrong hurt more than the beating. Crying, I held on to the piece of Sophie's hair with the yellow ribbon.

'I couldn't help it, Sophie,' I sobbed. 'I couldn't help it.'

12 The Inspector Comes to See Me

In the evening I grew calmer. I found that Rosalind was trying to send think-pictures to talk to me. Some of the others in our group were asking what was the matter, too. I told them about Sophie. It was not a secret now. I could feel that all of them were very shocked. I tried to say that a Mutant was not like a monster. And if you had something very small wrong with you, like Sophie, then you were hardly different from a Norm.

I knew they found that hard to believe. But they knew I was not lying – you cannot lie when you talk with your thoughts. They tried to understand what I was saying. But the idea was so new to them that they soon gave up and fell asleep.

It was a long time before I went to sleep. I lay thinking about Sophie and her parents. I wondered if they had reached the Fringes. Had they been caught because I had told the truth to my father?

When I did go to sleep I had the dream again of my father killing Sophie in the yard. I woke up shouting to him to stop. Then I fell asleep again. I dreamt again about the city by the sea. Once more I could see the houses and streets and the silver things that flew in the sky. It was a long time since I had had that dream but the city still looked just the same. When I woke up I felt better.

In the morning my mother came in, but she was very quiet and did not look pleased with me. Mary came in again and told me not to get up. I lay on my front. When Mary had gone I made plans for running away. I thought I would steal a horse and ride to the Fringes. I spent all morning thinking about running away.

In the afternoon, the inspector came in, with a bag of

sweets. He was friendly, but he had come to ask questions. He took a sweet and then he asked me:

'How long have you known that child – what is her name?'

I told him. There was no harm in that now.

'How long have you known that Sophie is a Mutant?'

'About six months, I think,' I told him.

The inspector looked serious.

'That is bad, you know,' he said. 'You must have known it was wrong not to tell anyone, didn't you?'

I did not look at him.

'It didn't seem as bad as they say in church,' I said. 'And they were very little toes.'

The inspector took another sweet and gave the bag back to me.

'Do you remember the law which says: "And each foot shall have five toes"?' he asked me.

'Yes,' I said, unhappily.

'Well, that little law is as important as any other. If a child does not follow the law by being a Norm, then it is not human. It is not in the image of God.'

He asked me why I hadn't told him or my father about Sophie. I told him about my dream – the one where my father killed Sophie because she was an Offence. The inspector thought for a while. Then he said:

'I should really report you for not telling anyone about Sophie. But as your father has beaten you, I may not have to report you. But you must remember that *anything* which makes someone different from a Norm is important. When we see a Mutant we must report it. Do you understand?'

I did not look at him. I said, 'Sophie was my friend.'

'It is a good thing to look after our friends,' said the inspector. 'But some things are more important. One day you will understand . . .' He stopped talking as the door opened. My father came in.

'They caught them – all three of them,' my father told

the inspector. My father looked as if he hated me. The inspector got up, and went out of the room with my father.

When they had gone, I could not help crying again. I felt that it was all my fault that Sophie and her parents had been caught. Perhaps if I had said nothing to my father, they would still be free. I forgot how my back hurt. The news my father had told the inspector was far worse than the beating.

Later the door opened. I kept my face to the wall. Steps crossed the room. A hand was put on my shoulder. The inspector's voice said :

'It wasn't your fault, old man. They were caught quite by chance, twenty miles away. They would have been caught even if you hadn't told your father what you knew.'

13   The Land Beyond the Badlands

Two days later, I said to Uncle Axel, 'I'm going to run away.' He stopped working and looked at his saw.

'I wouldn't do that,' he said. 'It doesn't usually work very well. Anyway, where would you run to ?'

'That's what I wanted to ask you,' I said.

He shook his head. 'It doesn't matter where you go,' he said. 'Wherever you are, people will want to see the paper that says you are a Norm. Then they will know who you are and where you are from.'

'Not in the Fringes,' I said.

Uncle Axel stared at me. 'Man alive, you don't want to go to the Fringes. They have got nothing there – not even enough food. Most of them are half-starving. That's why they come to attack us. You'd spend all your time trying to stay alive. And you'd be lucky if you did that,' he said.

'But there must be some other places,' I said.

'Not unless you can find a ship to take you, and even then . . .' said Uncle Axel. He shook his head again. 'If you run away from a place, you often don't like the place you go to, either,' he said. 'Running *to* a place is different, but where would you run to? Believe me, it is better here than in most places. I don't think you should go, David. Not now. Perhaps when you are a man you could go. If you went now they would find you and bring you back.'

I began to think Uncle Axel was right. I did not want to be caught and brought back to Waknuk. But it seemed that even when I was a man it would be hard to find a place to go to.

'What is the world outside Labrador like, Uncle Axel?' I asked.

'It is not like here, and it is a place where no one tries to please God,' he said. That was the kind of answer my father would give. I thought Uncle Axel would give a better one, and I told him so. He smiled.

'Well, if you don't tell everyone what I say, I will tell you what I know,' he said.

'Do you mean it is a secret?' I asked.

'No, it isn't a secret,' said Uncle Axel. 'But when people have believed for a long time that all the land beyond Labrador is Badlands, they don't want to hear anything different.'

'My book says it is all Badlands, or Fringes,' I said.

'Not all books say that. And I know things about the world because I have been on ships a long way from here. But you must not tell anyone what I tell you,' said Uncle Axel.

And then he told me many things, too many for me to remember all of them. But he told me that he had sailed up the river, south of Waknuk, to the sea. When you got to the

35

sea, there was no point in going north, or straight on to the east. If you went north you came to a very cold land, with only a few animals and birds – no people at all. And if you went east, the sea went on for ever. No one had ever reached the other side.

But if you went south you saw many things. If you kept close to the coast you could see that the land south of Labrador *was* all Badlands, for a very long way.

In the Badlands were Mutants worse than anyone had ever seen. They were mostly very strange plants, growing from the land into the sea. There was corn bigger than trees, and plants growing on rocks with long roots like hair, blown in the wind. There were plants that grew on the tops of cliffs and sent thick, green stems down more than a hundred feet, into the sea. They could have been plants growing from the land into the sea, or from the sea into the land – there was no way of telling. There were very few animals, and no people. There were only birds. It was a very strange, frightening place.

Then, if you went further south, you came to a place much worse. There, everything was black. The sea was dark, with no fish or plants. The coast was black and the cliffs were black. These Black Coasts seemed to go on for ever and very few ships had ever sailed very far down. But then Uncle Axel told me the most important thing. Some ships, quite a long time ago, had sailed further down. They had sailed past the Black Coasts. And they found a new land.

The ships came back to Labrador with gold, and silver and spices. And the sailors from these ships told the people in Labrador that there were people living in the new land. There were many different kinds of Mutants. In some places there were people with no hair. In other places everyone had white hair and pink eyes. In others the people looked just like the Norms in Labrador but were black.

But the strangest thing of all was that whatever the people were like, they thought that *they* were Norms. To them, all of the Norms in Labrador would look like Mutants. They had the same stories about the Old People that we had. But they were all sure that they were now in the true image of God and that everyone else was a Mutant.

When Uncle Axel had finished telling me all this about the south, I said :

'Uncle Axel, are there any cities in the south?' I told him about the city in my dream.

'No,' he said. 'There is no city like that.'

I was upset. I had thought that if I ran away I would find the city in my dream. But Uncle Axel was sure that there was no city in the world like the one in my dream.

Then Uncle Axel said, 'Do you understand, David, why I have told you all this? I'm telling you that nobody, *nobody,* knows what is the true image of God. Nobody really *knows* what a Norm is. How do I know that you and Rosalind are not Norms? We know that the Old People could talk to each other without seeing each other. Only you and Rosalind can do that now. Perhaps you are nearer to the true image than anyone else.'

I decided to tell Uncle Axel that there were others who could talk to each other in think-pictures.

'Others?' said Uncle Axel. 'Who are they? How many?' I shook my head.

'I don't know their names,' I said. 'Names do not have any think-pictures. We have never asked each other our names. I only found out who Rosalind was by accident.'

Uncle Axel looked very serious.

'How many are there of you?' he said again.

'Eight,' I told him. 'There were nine. But one of them stopped about a month ago. I wanted to ask you, Uncle Axel. Do you think someone found out, and killed one of us?'

Uncle Axel thought. Then he shook his head.

'I don't think anyone found out. We would all have

37

heard about it. Perhaps the one who has stopped talking has gone away,' he said.

'I am sure he would have told us if he was going away,' I said.

'Then I think he must have had an accident,' said Uncle Axel. 'I will try to find out anything I can.'

Then Uncle Axel left me. He told me again to think about what he had said : that no one knew what the true image was. He told me not to worry too much that Rosalind and I and the others were different. When he had gone, I thought I would not try to run away yet. It looked as if it would be very difficult.

Some months later, Uncle Axel told me that a boy called Walter had had an accident. He was helping to chop down trees, and one of them fell on him. It had happened at the same time as we had noticed that there were only eight of us. It seemed as if Walter must have been the boy like us who could talk thoughts in think-pictures. I was sorry he was dead, but I was glad we knew now what had happened. I was glad that we were still safe.

14   My Baby Sister

Some time after this my sister Petra was born. I was very surprised because I did not know that my mother was going to have a baby.

Everyone on the farm pretended to be very surprised too.

For about two weeks I had felt as if people were hiding something from me. But I didn't understand what it was.

Then, one night, I heard a baby crying. But in the morning no one said anything about a baby. When a baby was born the father had to go at once to the inspector. The inspector would come to inspect the baby. If it was a Norm, in the true image, he would give the parents a certificate. A certificate was the piece of paper saying that the baby was a Norm. A man as important as my father wanted his certificate as quickly as possible. If the baby was not a Norm, then everyone could pretend that it had never been born. That was why no one talked about the cries in the night.

As soon as it was light my father sent one of the farm men on a horse to tell the inspector to come. While we waited for him to come we tried to hide our worry. We pretended we were just starting another ordinary day. When the farm man came back, he did not bring the inspector with him. The inspector sent a message to say that he would try to call some time that day.

My father was very angry. And he knew that the inspector meant to make him angry. He spent the morning in the house and yard shouting at people. So everyone worked very hard, hoping that he would not notice them. We all pretended that my mother was in bed with a cold. The only person who went into her room was my sister Mary.

We were worried because twice before my mother had had a baby who had not been given a certificate. People wondered if my father would send my mother away if *this* baby was not a Norm.

At last the inspector came, in the middle of the afternoon. He seemed in no hurry, and walked slowly into the house, talking about the weather. My father found it hard to be polite, and was red in the face. He told Mary to take the inspector to my mother's room. Then we had the worst wait of all.

Mary said afterwards that the inspector took a long time to inspect the baby. He looked at her very carefully. Then he came down and went into the front room. He very slowly wrote the certificate which said that the baby was a Norm, in the true image. Then he looked at it. At last he wrote his name and put the date. Still looking worried, he gave the certificate to my father. My father was angry. He knew that if the inspector was *really* worried, he would ask another inspector to come and see the baby.

But now everyone could say that there was a new baby in the family. I was told I had a new sister and later I was taken to see her. She looked very pink. I did not know how the inspector could really tell that she was a Norm.

While we were taking turns to look at her, someone started to ring the stable bell. Everyone on the farm stopped work. Very soon we were all in the kitchen, saying prayers. We thanked God that Petra, my new sister, was a normal baby.

19   Aunt Harriet and Her Baby

Two or three days after Petra was born I found out something about my family. I did not like what I found out.

I was sitting quietly in the room next to my parents' room. My mother was still in bed. If I waited for half an hour after lunch, I could creep out and go away from the farm. If I did this I would not be given a job for the afternoon. This room was a good place to hide, but I had to keep very quiet. The wall between this room and the next was thin and cracked, and I had to move quietly in case my mother heard me.

That day, I was just thinking that I had been in the room long enough. Then I saw a horse and cart stop in the yard.

As it passed my window I saw my Aunt Harriet holding the reins of the horse.

I had only seen her a few times because she lived about fifteen miles away. But I liked her. She was my mother's sister. They looked alike, but Aunt Harriet had a softer face. She was easier to talk to than my mother.

I crept to the window. I saw Aunt Harriet get down from the cart and come into the house. She was carrying something. A few seconds later I heard her steps pass my door. She went into my mother's room.

'Hello, Harriet!' said my mother. She did not sound very pleased. 'So soon! Have you brought a tiny baby all that way?'

'I had to come, Emily, I had to,' said Aunt Harriet. 'I heard your baby had come early so I – oh, there she is! Oh she's lovely, Emily.'

There was silence. Then Aunt Harriet said, 'My baby is lovely too, isn't she? Isn't she a darling?'

I could hear them talking about each other's babies. Then my mother said, 'I *am* glad, my dear. Your husband must be very pleased.'

'Of course he is,' said Aunt Harriet. But there was something wrong with the way she said it. She went on quickly, 'My baby was born a week ago. I didn't know what to do. Then I heard your baby had come early and was a girl, too. It was like God answering a prayer.' Then she said, 'Have you got her certificate?'

'Of course,' said my mother, sharply. Then she said quickly, 'Harriet! Do you mean that your baby has not got a certificate?'

Aunt Harriet did not answer, but I thought I could hear her crying. My mother said, 'Harriet, let me see that baby – properly.'

For some seconds I could hear nothing but my aunt crying. Then she said, 'It's such a little thing, you see. It is nothing much.'

'*Nothing much!*' said my mother. 'You bring a monster like that into my house and say it is *nothing much*!'

'*Monster!*' cried Aunt Harriet. 'Oh, oh, oh . . .' She went on crying. My mother said:

'Why have you come here, Harriet? Why have you brought your baby here?'

Aunt Harriet blew her nose. Then she said in a dull, flat voice: 'I thought I could change my baby with yours for a few days. Just until I get the certificate.'

My mother took her breath in quickly.

'It would not be for long,' said Aunt Harriet. 'You are my sister, Emily – my sister. You are the only person in the world who can help me to keep my baby.' She began to cry again.

My mother said: 'In all my life I have never heard anything so wicked. I think you must be mad, Harriet. To think that I would change my baby for yours . . .' She stopped talking. She could hear my father coming.

When my father came in, my mother said to him: 'Send her away. Tell her to leave the house. And tell her to take *that* with her.'

My mother told him what had happened. Aunt Harriet did not speak. When my mother had stopped talking, my father said to Aunt Harriet:

'Is this story true? Is this why you have come here?'

Slowly, Aunt Harriet said: 'This is the third time I have had a baby who is a Mutant. The inspector will take my baby again. I can't stand that – not again. My husband will find another wife. There will be nothing in the world for me. I came here because Emily is my sister. I thought she would help. I can see now that I was wrong to hope . . .'

No one spoke.

'All right; I understand. I will go now,' said Aunt Harriet.

My father said, 'I do not understand how you dared to come here. What is worse, you do not seem to be sorry.'

Aunt Harriet answered, 'Why should I be sorry? I have done nothing wrong. I am not sorry – only beaten.'

'Not sorry!' said my father. 'You have tried to make your sister do something very wicked. God is angry with you, Harriet. You have been very wicked in your life. That is why you have given birth to a Mutant.'

'One poor little baby!' said Aunt Harriet.

'That baby would grow up and have children. The children would be Mutants too. Soon there would be Mutants all over the land. We must keep to the true image of the Old People. Now go! Tell the inspector that you have this baby. Then pray. Ask God to forgive you.'

I heard Aunt Harriet pick up her baby and go to the door. Then she said: 'Yes, I shall pray. I shall ask God to send love into the world. I shall ask if he really wants a little baby to die because it has something wrong with it. I shall ask God to punish people who think that they are always right . . .'

Then the door closed and I heard her walk down the stairs. I crept to the window. I saw Aunt Harriet put her baby into the cart and look at her. Then she climbed up into the cart and drove off. I shall never forget her eyes. They seemed to see nothing.

I could hear my father and mother talking. My father said again that Aunt Harriet was a very wicked woman.

My mother said, 'Perhaps she did not know what she was saying.'

'Then it is time she did know,' said my father.

My mother began to cry. I had never heard her cry before. I wondered what was wrong with Aunt Harriet's baby, but I never found out.

The next day I was told that Aunt Harriet's body had been found in the river. No one said anything about a baby.

16   I am Very Frightened

The evening we heard that Aunt Harriet was dead, my
father said prayers for her with the family. After that she
was never talked about again. It seemed as if everyone had
forgotten about her, except for me. I could not forget her
saying, 'I am not sorry – only beaten.' And I could not
forget her face when she left the house.

No one told me how she died, but I knew that it had not
been an accident. Somehow, her death worried me more
than anything that had ever happened before. I was afraid
– more afraid than when Sophie had been caught. For
several nights I dreamed of Aunt Harriet lying in the river,
holding her baby. And I was frightened . . .

Aunt Harriet had died just because her baby was
different from other babies. There was the 'little thing' that
made it not quite right . . . A Mutant, my father had called
it. A Mutant! I remembered the words I had heard in
church: *Look out for the Mutant! The Mutant is
wicked!* Such a small thing made you a Mutant . . .

I began to pray very hard every night.

'Oh, God,' I said, 'please, please, God, let me be like other
people. I don't want to be different. I want to wake up in
the morning and find I am like other people. *Please*, God!'

And every morning I tested myself. But I found I could
still talk with think-pictures to Rosalind and the others. I
had to go on being the same person. I had to go on seeing
the notices in the house :

The Mutant is wicked! God hates the Mutant!

And I went on being very frightened.

After I had been praying for about five nights, Uncle Axel
asked me to work with him one morning. We were mending

a plough, a big spade pulled by horses to dig the earth. When we had been working for about two hours Uncle Axel said we could rest. He gave me some cake and we sat eating in the sun. Then he said :

'Well now, David, what is it?'

'What do you mean?' I asked.

'You have been looking quite ill for the last few days. Why are you worried? Has someone found out that you can talk with thoughts?'

'No,' I said. Uncle Axel looked very pleased.

'But what *is* the matter?' he asked.

So I told him about Aunt Harriet and the baby. Before I had finished I was crying. It felt so good to tell someone all about what had happened.

When I had finished I looked up at Uncle Axel. His face was very sad and hard.

'So that was it,' he said.

'It was just because the baby was different,' I said. 'And there was Sophie too . . . I didn't understand before. I'm frightened, Uncle Axel. What will they do when they find out I'm different?'

He put his hand on my shoulder.

'No one else is ever going to know,' he told me. 'No one knows except me, and I won't tell anyone. There is nothing to show that you are different. Learn to watch yourself, David, and they will never find out.'

'What *did* they do to Sophie?' I asked, but Uncle Axel would not answer that. He went on :

'Remember what I told you. They *think* they are the true image. But they cannot know for sure. And even if they are the same as the Old People, what does it matter? Where are the Old People now? Where is their wonderful world?'

'God sent the Tribulation to them,' I said.

'It is easy just to say that. But we don't even really understand what the Tribulation was. It was worse than a storm, worse than fire and even worse than an earthquake. It was like all three together, and something a lot worse, too. It made the Black Coasts, and the Badlands. And *why* did it happen? I don't understand why God sent such a terrible thing. I don't understand why he allows Mutants and Offences to keep coming into the world,' said Uncle Axel.

I tried to say that God could do anything he liked, without giving the reason.

'That is not good enough, David,' said Uncle Axel. 'We must believe that God is good. And if God was good he would not have allowed the world to go so wrong. So why did we have the Tribulation? And is it right that we should go on trying to make the world as it was when the Old People were alive? It is clear, David, that however wonderful the Old People were, they still made mistakes.'

It was hard to understand him, but I said:

'But, Uncle Axel, if we don't try to be like the Old People, and keep everyone in the true image, what *can* we do?'

'We could try to be ourselves,' said Uncle Axel. 'We could try to live in *this* world, and not always think about the past. What do you think makes a man?'

I started to say what I had been taught: 'The Norm is the image of God . . .'

'But a doll could be in the image of God,' said my uncle. 'What makes man different from everything else is that man has a mind. That is the most important thing we have. You and Rosalind and the others have different minds from everyone else. But that does not mean that your minds are bad. If you have been praying to God to make your mind like everyone else's, you are wrong. It is like asking God to make you deaf or blind. You must face the fact that you are different, David. And you must try to use the fact that you are different, but still keep yourself safe.'

46

That evening I talked to Rosalind and the others. We thought we should all know each other's names now. If we knew that, we should not have to wonder so much if someone stopped talking. We would know who it was. There were eight of us : Rosalind and I and six others. The others were Michael, who lived about three miles to the north, Sally and Katherine who lived on two farms further away, Mark, almost nine miles away in the north-west, and Anne and Rachel. Anne and Rachel were sisters. They lived on a farm only about a mile to the west. Anne was the eldest. She was thirteen.

Now that we knew how many there were of us and we knew each other's names, we all felt much safer. After a time I found that I did not worry so much about the notices in the house saying *Look Out for the Mutant!* And I did not think so often about Aunt Harriet and Sophie.

I had many new things to think about. Michael went to a much better school than the rest of us. He taught us far more than we learnt at school. He did not really understand some of the things he told us. But when we had all thought about them, they got much easier to understand. It was good to feel that I was learning all the time. But I had to be careful not to let anyone outside our group guess how I had learnt new things. We all had to be careful. It was not easy. We had to keep quiet when people said things that we knew were wrong. But somehow we did it.

For six years we felt safe. Until the day when we found that the eight of us had suddenly become nine.

17 Petra In Danger

It was a funny thing about my little sister, Petra. She was now six years old, and she seemed so normal. She was a very pretty little girl. Everyone loved her. I never thought there was anything different about her. Until the day it happened . . .

It was summer. Twelve of us men were harvesting in a big field, getting in all the corn. I had just given my knife to another man, and I was tying up some corn. One moment I was tying up the long corn. The next moment I felt as if something had hit me inside my head. I felt a great pain. Then I felt as if something was pulling inside my head. I knew I had to follow the pulling. I dropped the corn and ran. Everyone looked very surprised.

I ran and ran, over the fields, to the river. When I had nearly got to the river I saw Rosalind. She was running like the wind. I went on running, to the deepest part of the river.

When I got there I jumped into the water. I saw Petra. She was in the deep water, holding on to a little bush. The bush was on the bank. The bush was bent into the water and the roots had nearly come away from the bank.

I swam to Petra and took her in my arms. Suddenly the pain in my head stopped. I carried Petra to a place where the water was not so deep. Then I stood up. I saw Rosalind on the bank. She looked very worried.

'Who is it?' she said. She spoke aloud. 'Who was able to do that? Who gave us that feeling in the head, and pulled us here?'

I told her that Petra had done it.

'*Petra?*' she said. She looked very surprised.

I carried my little sister to the bank. I put her down on

the grass. She was very tired, but she was alive. Rosalind came over. We looked down at Petra. Her dress and her hair were very wet. Rosalind and I looked at each other.

'I didn't know,' I said. 'I didn't know she was one of us.'

Rosalind shook her head.

'She isn't one of us,' she said. 'She is like us. But she is much stronger than us. None of us could *command* like that. She is something much more than we are.'

Now other people came up. Some came from my farm, some came from Rosalind's farm. They had seen us running. I picked up Petra to take her home. One of the men from my farm looked at me.

'But how did you know?' he asked. 'I did not hear a thing.'

Rosalind turned to him. She looked very surprised.

'You didn't hear her?' she said. 'You must be deaf! She was calling very loudly.'

The man shook his head. He looked as if he did not believe her. But Rosalind and I both said we had heard Petra calling. So the man did not ask any more questions.

That night, for the first time for years, I had my old dream. It was the dream where my father killed Sophie, because she was a Mutant. But this time I dreamed that he killed Petra. I woke up very afraid ...

The next day, I tried to send think-pictures to Petra. I knew it was important that she did not tell anyone what she could do. I could not get an answer from her. The others all tried too. They could not get an answer either.

I said to Rosalind :

'Perhaps I should tell her in ordinary words.'

'No,' said Rosalind. 'If she does not know what she can do we must not worry her. She is only six. It is better to wait until we have to tell her.'

49

All the others thought Rosalind was right. We thought we would not tell Petra anything about think-pictures until she was older. We must keep on hiding what we knew from everyone else.

As we all grew up, we learnt more about the world we lived in. We found that we were really in great danger. As Michael said, we had been given a gift, because we could talk in think-pictures. But it was more like a curse.

The summer before this one, many of the plants and animals had been Offences and Mutants. I heard Jacob, one of the old men on the farm, talking about it. He said that it was because we were wicked that we had so many Mutants that summer. He said that people were too kind to human Mutants.

'If a baby is a Mutant it should be burnt,' he said. 'The Mutant is a wicked thing. If we let it live, and let it go into the Fringes, we are wrong. We should kill it at once. God is angry with us because we have let Mutants go on living. That is why we are having such a bad summer. That is why so many plants are Offences and Mutants this year.'

I asked Uncle Axel if many people still thought the same as Jacob.

'Some of the older people do. We don't know why we are getting so many Mutant plants and animals this summer. Perhaps it is something to do with the weather. But people listen to the old men when they talk like that. If next summer is bad as well, they will think the old men are right. Then they will look very hard for human Mutants. So be careful.'

Uncle Axel was right. This summer was a bad one. There were many things wrong with the plants and animals. People were very angry if they heard that anyone had hidden a Mutant. So we were worried in case anyone found out about Petra.

But people soon stopped talking about Petra in the river.

We felt safe for a time. But a month later we were very worried. Anne, one of our group, said that she was going to marry . . .

18   Anne Falls in Love

Anne would not change her mind. She was nineteen now, and wanted to marry Alan. Alan was the boy who had seen Sophie's footprint and had told the inspector. Anne's parents had a big farm. They wanted Anne to marry Alan because he was strong and could help on the farm. We were very worried.

Michael talked in think-pictures to Anne first.

'You cannot marry Alan,' he said. 'It will be like marrying someone who cannot walk. Think what it will be like.'

Anne was angry. 'I am not a fool,' she said. 'Of course I have thought. I have thought more than any of you. There are three men and five women in our group. That means that two women will have to marry Norms. I love Alan and I am going to marry him.'

'But perhaps there are more of us,' said Michael. 'Perhaps there are others we do not know about. If we wait . . .'

'How long must we wait?' said Anne. 'I have Alan now. You want me to give him up. Perhaps I will never find someone else like us. None of you have thought about that. None of you are in love, except David and Rosalind. So you don't know what it is like.'

It was true that we had never really thought about marriage. But we all thought about it now. We all knew that we could never marry Norms. It would mean keeping a secret all our lives. It would be like living with someone whom you could never talk to properly. And one day the secret would come out.

Anne knew this. But she would not talk about it. Soon, we found that we could not talk to her. She shut off her mind from us.

Rosalind and I talked about what had happened. We did not know what to do. It was true that we were in love. Rosalind was now a tall, slim young woman. She was very pretty, and many of the men in Waknuk wanted to marry her. But she did not want any of them.

It was difficult for us to meet, because my father and Uncle Angus, her father, hated each other. We had to make love in secret. We wondered if we would ever be able to marry. But we knew that meeting in secret was better than marrying a Norm. Rosalind was very shocked that Anne was going to marry Alan.

I talked to Uncle Axel. He knew that Anne and Alan were going to marry. But he did not know that Anne was one of us. When I told him he looked worried. Then he said :

'You are right, David. They must not marry. It is too dangerous. Are you telling me because you don't know what to do?'

'Yes,' I said. 'Anne will not talk to us any more. We think she is trying to pretend that she is a Norm. She is trying to forget that she can talk in think-pictures. She told us that she hated all of us. She wants to marry Alan and she doesn't care what will happen.'

'Do you think perhaps she *can* live like a Norm?' asked Uncle Axel.

'She can try,' I said. 'But it would be like living in silence. We don't think she will be able to live all her life like that. But what can we do?' I asked.

'Do you think it would be right to kill Anne?' said Uncle Axel. 'If she marries Alan you will all be in danger. It is too big a secret for Anne to keep. One day she will need help, and tell Alan. But if she dies, the rest of you will be safe.'

'No!' I said. 'We could not do that. We are all very close. I love Anne more than my own family. It is difficult to tell you . . .' I stopped. 'It would be like killing a part of ourselves.'

'If you do not kill her, you will always be in danger,' said Uncle Axel.

'It would be better to be in danger than to kill her,' I said. But I was very unhappy.

19   Anne and Alan Get Married

I could not tell any of the others what Uncle Axel had said. There was a chance that Anne would pick up our thoughts. But I knew that they would think I was right. We could not kill Anne. There was nothing we could do.

Anne did not send any more think-pictures. Rachel, her sister, told us that Anne was trying to live like a Norm. The day came when Anne and Alan were married. They went to live in a house on Anne's farm.

For some months we heard nothing. Anne did not like Rachel to go and see her. It seemed as if she was trying to cut off from all of us. All we could do was hope that she was happy. And we hoped that she would never tell Alan about us.

Rosalind and I thought a lot when Anne and Alan got married. Neither of us could remember when we had first known that *we* would get married. It seemed as if we had always known it. When two people can talk to each other as Rosalind and I could, and when there is danger all around, they need each other even before they know they are in love. But when we knew that we were in love, we knew that the feeling was no different from how a Norm would feel. We knew we had the same difficulties as Norms . . .

My father still hated Uncle Angus, Rosalind's father. Uncle Angus still hated my father. Even if Rosalind and I had been Norms, with no other danger, it would have been difficult to marry. We knew that our families would never let us. Rosalind's mother was looking for other men for Rosalind to marry. I saw my mother looking at girls for me.

We went on meeting in secret.

After six months, we all got used to being afraid. We heard nothing from Anne. So we began to feel safer. It seemed as if nothing would happen.

Then, one Sunday evening, Alan was found dead. He was lying near his home with an arrow in his neck.

We heard the news from Rachel. We all listened as she tried to talk to Anne. But there was no answer. Even though Anne was unhappy, she would not talk in think-pictures.

'I am going to see her,' said Rachel. 'She must have someone with her.'

We all waited for over an hour. Then Rachel talked to us.

'Anne will not see me,' said Rachel. 'She will not let me into the house. She has let someone else in from the next house, but she will not let me in to the house. She shouted at me and told me to go away.'

'Anne must think that one of us killed Alan,' said Michael. 'Did any of you kill him?'

One after another we all said that we had not killed Alan.

'You must write Anne a note,' Michael told Rachel. 'You must tell her that we did not kill Alan. Write so that she will understand, but no one else will know what you mean. Be careful.'

'I will try,' said Rachel.

We waited for another hour. Then we heard Rachel again.

'It is no good,' she said. 'I gave the note to the woman who is with Anne. The woman said that Anne tore up the note. Now my mother is in the house with Anne. My mother wants her to come home.'

We were all silent. Then Michael said :

'We may have to run away. We must all get ready, but we must be very careful. Rachel, you must go on trying to talk to Anne. Let us know what happens.'

Everyone on the farm had gone to bed when we heard Rachel again.

'Mother and I are going home now,' said Rachel. 'Anne will not come with us. She has made us go away. She told Mother that she knows who killed Alan. But she did not say who it was.'

'Are you sure she thinks it was us?' said Michael. 'Perhaps Alan had a row with someone else who killed him.'

'No,' said Rachel, 'I am sure she thinks it was one of us. If she did not think that she would let me in. I will go to see her again in the morning.'

So there was nothing we could do for the rest of the night.

20   Poor Anne

Rachel told us later what happened in the morning. She had got up very early and walked over the fields to Anne's house. She knocked on the door. There was silence. She knocked again. There was still no answer.

She went to the house next door. The woman came with her to Anne's house. They pushed in a window with some wood. They climbed through the window. They went upstairs. They found Anne in her bedroom, hanging from a rope in the ceiling.

They cut the rope and put Anne on her bed. She was dead. Rachel was very shocked. The woman from the house next door put a sheet over Anne. The woman took Rachel's arm to take her out of the house. As they were going the woman saw a note on the table.

'This will be for you, or your parents,' said the woman.

Rachel looked at the note. It was addressed to the inspector. 'But it is not . . .' Rachel said. Then she stopped. She saw that the woman could not read. 'Oh, I see, it is for my parents. I will give it to them,' said Rachel.

The woman took Rachel back to her family's farm. There, Rachel told her parents that Anne was dead. Then she went to her room. She read the note that Anne had left for the inspector.

The note said that we could all talk in think-pictures. It even told the inspector about Petra. It said that we had all planned to kill Alan. It said that one of us had killed him, but it did not say who.

Rachel read the note twice. Then she carefully burnt it.

No one outside our group wondered why Anne had killed herself. She was going to have a baby. Everyone thought that she had been so unhappy when Alan died that she had gone mad. They thought it was very sad, but they thought they could understand it.

But no one could understand who had killed Alan. For some weeks everyone talked about it. The arrow that had killed him belonged to an old man called William Tay. But he made all the arrows in Waknuk. So that did not prove anything. Everyone tried to think of people who wanted to kill Alan. But they could not think of anyone. A story went round that Anne had not really loved Alan. People said that she had killed him and then killed herself. But no one could really find a reason for that. At last they stopped talking about it.

None of us knew who had killed Alan. We were sad that Anne was dead. But we had not been able to talk to her for a long time before she died. Now she was dead, we were safe.

Only Michael went on being worried. He said:

'One of us was not strong enough . . .'

21 Petra Calls For Help

That year, the young plants and the animals born in the spring were nearly all Norms. People were very pleased. They had killed the Mutant plants and animals last year. Now it looked as if they had done the right thing. They were very happy and friendly to each other.

The weather was very good. It looked as if we were going to have a good summer. Rosalind and I and the others worked hard on our farms. We all felt safe. And then something happened to Petra . . .

It was one day early in June. Petra did two things that she knew were wrong. She rode her pony off our own land. And she went into the woods. The woods were supposed to be fairly safe. But it was wrong to go there without a weapon. There were wild cats and larger animals which are dangerous.

Suddenly I could feel that Petra was calling. It was very like the call she had given from the river. It was very strong.

I tried to get through to the others. But Petra's call was so strong that I could not reach them. I could not tell why she was calling. I just knew that something was very wrong.

I ran to get my gun. In a few minutes I was on my horse. I did not know why Petra was calling, but I knew she was in the woods. I rode there as fast as I could.

If Petra had stopped calling for just a little while I could have talked to the others. But she did not. There was nothing to do except go to her.

The land near the woods was very rough. Once I fell off my horse. Then I got into the woods. I had to find the path that led to Petra. She was calling all the time. At last I found the right path. The trees were very close together. The branches were very low. But I kept on. At last I reached a clearing.

At first I did not see Petra. I saw her pony lying on the ground. Its throat was torn open. An animal was eating one of the pony's legs. It was tearing at the flesh with its teeth.

The animal was the strangest I had ever seen. It was brown, with dark brown and yellow spots. It had very big feet, with long claws. Its feet were covered with blood. Its face was round and it had eyes like yellow glass. It had very big teeth.

I took my gun from my back. The movement made the animal stop tearing at the pony's body. It turned its head and sat very still, looking at me. Blood shone on its mouth. Its tail rose, and waved from side to side. I raised the gun. Suddenly, an arrow came through the air. It hit the animal in the throat. The animal jumped into the air, then landed on all fours. It faced me, with its yellow eyes shining. My horse was very frightened. It jumped up and my gun went off. But before the animal could jump at me, two more arrows came through the trees. One hit the animal in the leg, another hit it in the head. It stood very still. Then it fell down dead.

Rosalind rode into the clearing. She was carrying a bow,

the weapon for shooting arrows. Then Michael came in. He was carrying a bow too. He looked at the animal to make sure it was dead.

We knew that Petra was very near. We could still see her in our thoughts.

'Where is she?' Rosalind asked in words.

We looked round. Then we saw Petra. She was about twelve feet up a tree, clinging to the trunk. Rosalind rode under the tree and told her it was safe to come down, but Petra did not move. I got off my horse and climbed up the tree. I helped her get down to Rosalind. Rosalind put her on her own horse and tried to calm her. But Petra was looking at her dead pony. Her thoughts were very unhappy, and she was still sending very strong think-pictures. 'We must stop this,' I said to Rosalind. 'Petra will bring all the others here.'

Michael came over. He looked at Petra. He said: 'She does not know she is sending such strong think-pictures. She is screaming with fright inside. It would be better for her to cry aloud. Let's take her away from her pony.'

We moved behind some bushes. Michael spoke to Petra quietly. But it did not help. We could still feel her unhappy thoughts.

'Let's all try at the same time to send calm think-pictures to her,' I said.

'Ready?'

We tried, for a full fifteen seconds. For just a moment Petra stopped being so unhappy. Then we could feel her thoughts again, just as strongly.

'No good,' said Rosalind, and she stopped.

We all looked at Petra. We were very worried. Her think-pictures were not so frightened now. But she was still very upset. At last she began to cry. Rosalind put an arm round her and held her close.

'Let her cry,' said Michael. 'It will do her good.'

We waited for her to calm down. And then Rachel came

riding out of the trees. A moment later a boy rode up as well. I had never seen him, but I knew he must be Mark.

We had never met as a group before. We knew that it would be dangerous. We were sure that Sally and Katherine, the other two girls, would be here soon. Michael, Rosalind and I quickly explained in words what had happened. We told Rachel and Mark to go away. We must not be found in a group. So they went away, and Michael went with them. They all went towards different places. Rosalind and I stayed with Petra.

About ten minutes later Sally and Katherine came up. They were on horses and carried bows and arrows. They looked at Petra. They were very surprised that she had given such a strong call. Rosalind and I told Sally and Katherine they must go away quickly. They were just about to go. Suddenly a large man rode into the clearing. He stopped his horse and looked at us.

'What is going on here?' he asked.

22   The Stranger in the Woods

I had never seen the man before. I did not like the look of him. I asked him to show me his papers. He showed them to me and I showed him mine.

'What is going on here?' he asked again.

I wanted to tell him to mind his own business. But I told him that my sister's pony had been attacked by a wild animal. I said that we had heard her calling and come to help her. He did not seem to believe me. He looked at me and then turned to Sally and Katherine.

'And why did you two come here so quickly?' he asked them.

'Of course we came when we heard the child calling,' said Sally.

'I was right behind you. I did not hear any calls,' said the man. Sally and Katherine looked at each other.

'Well, *we* heard calls,' said Sally.

I said: 'I would have thought everyone could hear the calls. The pony was screaming too, poor thing.'

I led the man round the bushes. I showed him the dead pony and the dead animal. He looked surprised. But he still thought there was something strange going on. He asked to see Rosalind's and Petra's papers.

'What is all this about?' I asked him.

'Didn't you know that there are Fringes people in the woods now?' said the man.

'No, I didn't,' I said. 'Anyway, do we *look* like Fringes people?'

He did not answer that. He said, ' Well, there are Fringes people around. There is going to be trouble. You should keep out of the woods.' He then looked at the pony again and then at Sally.

'I don't think this pony can have screamed for at least half an hour,' he said. 'Why did you two come straight to this spot?'

'Well,' said Sally, 'We knew this was the place where the screams were coming from. When we got nearer we heard the little girl calling.'

'It was very good of you to come,' I said to them quickly. 'If we hadn't been here you would have saved Petra's life. Thank you. I will take her home now. Goodbye.'

Sally and Katherine said goodbye quickly. They said they hoped Petra would soon be all right. Then they rode off.

The man still looked as if he thought there was something wrong. But there was nothing he could do. He looked at Rosalind and Petra and me again, very hard. Then he told us again to keep out of the woods, and he rode off. We watched him go.

'Who is he?' asked Rosalind. She sounded very worried.

I knew from the man's papers that his name was Jerome Skinner. But I knew nothing else about him. I tried to ask Sally if she knew anything else. But Petra's thoughts were still in my mind and I could not get through to anyone else.

We took Petra home. My mother put her to bed. At last, at nine o'clock, she fell asleep. Then we could all talk to each other again. Rosalind and I asked the others if they knew who Jerome Skinner was. Sally said:

'He is new here. My father knows him. He has a farm very close to the woods. That is why he saw us riding to you.'

'Why do you think he did not believe us?' asked Rosalind. 'Do you think he knows anything about think-pictures?'

'No,' said Sally. 'I tried to send thoughts to him. But he did not get them.'

Michael started to join in. We asked him if he thought that Norms knew about think-pictures. He said, 'Some of them do have an idea that it may be possible, but they don't really understand how. They call it telepathy. But most of them don't believe in it at all.'

Rosalind said, 'That man looked as if he knew something. Has anyone else been asking questions?'

We all said no.

'Good,' said Rosalind. 'But we must be careful that this doesn't happen again. David will have to tell Petra about think-pictures. He will have to tell her in words. If any of you hear her calling like that again, do not take any notice. David or I will go to Petra if she calls. We must never meet as a group again. Do you all understand?'

Everyone said yes. Then the others said goodbye. Rosalind and I talked about Petra. Somehow we had to tell her about think-pictures. We must make her understand what she could do.

23 Teaching Petra about Think-Pictures

I woke early the next morning. I could feel Petra's thoughts again. She was still unhappy, but her thoughts were not so strong today. I tried to talk to her. I could tell that she was listening. But she did not know what was happening. I got out of bed and went along to her room. She was glad to see me and I could feel her thoughts get happier. I said I would take her fishing in the afternoon.

When we went fishing I talked to her. I tried to explain that some people could talk in think-pictures. I tried to tell her that she could do it too, even though she did not know what she was doing. I tried to tell her that her calls were stronger than anyone else's. But Petra did not understand. She got tired of listening to me. So I said:

'Let's play a game. You shut your eyes. Keep them shut. Now pretend you are looking down a deep, deep hole. You cannot see anything except dark. Right?'

'Yes,' said Petra. Her eyes were tight shut.

'Good,' I said. 'Now, don't think of anything at all. Just look at the dark. Now watch!'

I made a think-picture of a rabbit. I made it twitch its nose. Petra smiled. Well, that was good. It proved she *could* pick up other people's think-pictures. I stopped thinking about the rabbit. I thought about a puppy, then some hens, then a horse. After a minute or two Petra opened her eyes.

'Where are they?' she said.

'They aren't anywhere. They were just think-pictures,' I told her. 'That is the game. Now I will shut my eyes too. We'll both look down the hole and think about the dark.

Then you think of something, so that I can see it.'

I made my mind very open. That was a mistake. Suddenly there was a big flash. I felt as if I had been hit on the head. Then the others all began to talk. They sounded very surprised. I told them what was going on.

'Well, be careful!' said Michael. 'I nearly put an axe through my foot.'

'I've burnt my hand on the kettle,' said Katherine.

'Calm her down,' said Rosalind.

I turned to Petra. 'You are too rough,' I said. 'This time, make a *little* think-picture. Do it very slowly and softly.'

Petra nodded and shut her eyes again.

'Here it comes!' I told the others.

This time Petra's thought was not so strong. It was still very bright, but I could see her think-picture. 'It is a fish!' I said. Petra laughed. 'Now *you* show *me*,' she said. We went on with the game.

The next afternoon we played the game again. It took a long time. Petra's thoughts were still very strong, but she was learning to keep them smaller and not so bright or loud. Later in the game, I said, 'Now Rosalind is going to give you a think-picture.'

'Where's Rosalind?' Petra asked, looking round.

'She is not here, but that doesn't matter with think-pictures,' I said. 'Now, look at the dark. Do not think about anything.'

We waited.

Rosalind made a pond. She put in ducks. They were funny ducks, all different colours. They did a little dance on the pond, but one duck kept going wrong. Petra loved it.

The fourth time we played the game, Petra was getting good at it. She learnt how to clear her mind without shutting her eyes. At the end of a week she had learnt a lot. She could send simple think-pictures to us. She could understand simple think-pictures if one of us sent them.

But she could not understand when we all talked together.

'It is too difficult to see all at once. And it is too quick,' she said. 'I can tell if it is you, or Rosalind doing it. And I can tell Michael and Sally. But the others are very difficult.'

'Which others?' I asked. 'Do you mean Katherine and Mark?'

'Oh no,' she said. 'The other ones. The ones a long way away.'

I kept calm.

'I don't think I know them. Who are they?' I asked.

'I don't know,' she said. 'Can't you hear them? They are over there, but a long, long way.' She pointed to the south.

I thought about what she had said.

'Are they there now?' I asked.

'Yes, but not much,' said Petra.

I tried to hear them. I could not hear anything.

'Try and send me think-pictures about them,' I said.

Petra tried, but I could not understand them. Petra found it difficult so we stopped.

Over the next few days Petra learnt more and more about think-pictures. We all felt very pleased. We knew that because she could send very strong think-pictures she was very important.

Michael said : 'This is going to be very interesting. But she must not tell anyone about it.'

24   Uncle Axel Gives Me a Warning

About ten days after this Uncle Axel asked me to go and help him mend a wheel. It was after supper, but it was still light. I knew he wanted to talk to me. We went out of the house. We went behind a pile of hay. Uncle Axel looked at me hard.

'Have you been careless, David?' he asked.

I knew what he meant. He was asking if there was any way that people could know I talked in think-pictures.

'No, I don't think so,' I told him.

'Have any of the others been careless?' said Uncle Axel. Again, I did not think so.

'Then why has Joe Darley been asking questions about you and Rosalind?' asked Uncle Axel.

'I have no idea,' I said.

Uncle Axel shook his head. 'I don't like it, boy. When the inspector wants to find things out, he asks Joe Darley. Joe always seems to find things out. I don't like it,' he said.

I said, 'But no one knows about think-pictures. There is a list of all the things which are not normal. Think-pictures are not on that list. So no one could say we were Mutants.'

'But everyone knows that there are things which are not normal that are not on that list. People find out new kinds of Mutants. If they think there is something strange about you and the others they will still say you are Mutants,' said Uncle Axel.

'If anyone asks questions I know what we will do,' I said. 'We will pretend we don't know what they are talking about. Then we will sound like Norms,' I said.

Uncle Axel was still worried.

'Rachel was very sad when her sister Anne died,' he said. 'Do you think she would have told anyone anything?'

'No,' I said. 'We would know if she had.'

'Well,' said Uncle Axel. 'What about Petra?'

I looked at him.

'How did you know about Petra?' I asked. 'I never told you about her.'

Uncle Axel nodded. 'So she *can* talk in think-pictures. I thought she could.'

'How did you find out? Did she tell you?' I asked. I wondered if anyone else had found out.

'No, she didn't tell me,' said my uncle. 'I knew because Anne told Alan. She told him about all of you. Some women are never happy until they are slaves for their husbands. That's the kind of woman she was. Maybe she did not mean to tell him. But she did.'

I was shocked. 'How do you know?' I asked.

Uncle Axel said: 'I knew because of the look on Alan's face. One day I saw him in church. He was looking first at Rosalind, then Rachel, then at you and Petra. The way he looked I could tell that he knew. And I did not like the look on his face. I knew that he would make you pay him to keep quiet.'

I asked, 'What did you do?'

'I went home and thought about it. Then I took my bow and arrow, and went out,' said my uncle.

'So it was *you* who killed Alan!' I said.

'It was the only thing to do, David. I knew that Anne might think that one of you killed Alan. But I had to do it.'

We went on talking for a while. Then I said:

'But why have people been asking questions about us *now*? Do you think it is anything to do with Petra and her dead pony?'

I told Uncle Axel all about what had happened in the woods. I told him about the man called Jerome Skinner. Uncle Axel said he would try to find out more about him.

That night we all talked in think-pictures. I told the others that Joe Darley had been asking questions about us. Michael said :

'I think it must have been Jerome Skinner, the man in the woods, who started everything. Now listen. We must make plans. We may need to run away. We live in different places. That means that David, Rosalind and Petra are in one group, Sally and Katherine are in the other. Jerome Skinner did not see Rachel or Mark or me. So we are all right at the moment. You must all be very careful. And listen to this, David : they must *never* catch Petra, *never*! If we think they are after her, we must kill her. It is kinder for her. If you do not kill her she will give us all away. And then they will send us all into the Fringes. They will hurt us so that none of us can have children. Do you all understand?'

Everyone said yes. I thought about Petra, hurt and unhappy in the Fringes. I knew it would be kinder to kill her. But I hoped we would never have to do that. So I said yes.

'Good,' said Michael. 'Now, Rosalind and David : make plans to run away. And Sally and Katherine too. I will try to find out what is going on.'

Before I went to bed I put some bread and cheese in a bag, and I put a bow and arrows by my bed. Then I got into bed. I lay there making plans. We would need clothes, and blankets, and water. I was still making my list when I fell asleep.

25 Running Away

About three hours later I woke up. My door was open. There was no moon that night. But there were stars. I could see Petra in the door. She was wearing her white nightdress. 'David,' she said. 'Rosalind...'

She did not need to go on. I could hear Rosalind at once.

'David,' she said, 'we must get away at once. They have caught Sally and Katherine...'

Michael spoke: 'Hurry up, both of you, while there is still time. They will try to catch you at the same time, before we can warn you. They got to Sally's and Katherine's homes at the same time. *Hurry!*'

'I will meet you by the mill,' said Rosalind to me. 'Be quick!'

I said to Petra in words, 'Get dressed quickly. Be very quiet.' Petra nodded. She could not understand all our think-pictures, but she knew that something was very wrong. She went out of the room. I dressed quickly and took my bedclothes. I found the bag of food and the bow and arrows. Then I went to Petra's room. She was nearly dressed. I took some clothes from her cupboard.

'Don't put on your shoes,' I said. 'Carry them and come quietly, like a cat.'

When we got outside, we put on our shoes. Petra started to speak, but I gave her the think-picture of Sheba, my horse. She nodded. We crept across the yard. I opened the stable door and heard a noise. I stopped to listen.

'Horses,' said Petra.

It *was* horses. I could hear them coming towards the farm. There was no time to put a saddle on Sheba. I led her out by a rope. I got up on to a box and and then on to Sheba. Petra got up behind me and put her arms round me.

Quietly, we went out of the yard and went down the path to the river. I could hear the horses getting near to the farm.

'Are you away?' I asked Rosalind.

'I have been away for ten minutes,' said Rosalind. 'I was all ready to go. We tried to talk to you a long time ago.'

Then she tried to talk to Sally and Katherine. They answered together. 'We are being taken to the inspector. We are pretending that we don't know why, or what is happening. Is that best?'

'Yes,' said Michael and Rosalind.

Sally went on, 'We think it is easier if we shut off our minds from you. Then it will be easier to act like Norms. So don't try to talk to us.'

'All right,' said Rosalind. 'But we shall be ready if you want to talk to us. Come on, David, I can see lights at your farm now.'

I looked back. Up at the house I could see a light in a window. I heard a man's voice. We had got to the river bank. I made Sheba trot. Soon we were near the mill. And then I knew we were near Rosalind. A few moments later I saw something move in the trees. I rode towards them. There was Rosalind. She had brought Uncle Angus's two big horses. They rose above us in the dark. Both of them had large baskets on their backs. Rosalind was in one of the baskets. She was holding her bow and arrow.

I rode up to her.

'Give me the blankets,' she said. 'What have you got in the sack?'

I told her I had got bread and cheese.

'Is that all?' she said.

'I was in such a hurry,' I said.

Rosalind put the blankets on her horse's back inside the basket. Then I helped Petra to get on top of them.

'We must keep together,' said Rosalind. 'There is room for you in the other basket.' She threw a rope ladder over the horse and I got off Sheba's back. 'Go on,' I said to Sheba. 'Go home.' She went off and I climbed up the ladder into the basket. Then we rode off. The second big horse was behind us, on a rope.

We trotted for a while. We left the path and followed a stream. The ground was wet. We slowed down and after some time we reached a place where the ground was hard and rocky. I knew then that Rosalind had made careful plans. People would not be able to see the horses' footprints.

Rosalind read my thought. 'It is a pity *you* didn't plan more and sleep less. My mother and I were packing for two hours. You were asleep all that time.'

'Your mother?' I asked. 'Does she *know*?'

'She guessed,' said Rosalind. 'We never talked about think-pictures, but she knew. When I told her we were running away she cried. But she helped me get ready.'

I thought about what she had said. I did not think my own mother would have helped me or Petra. But she had cried about Aunt Harriet. And Aunt Harriet had been ready to hide her Mutant baby. So had Sophie's mother. I wondered how many other mothers felt the same.

We went on riding. There were more rocky places and more streams. At last the sky went grey. We rode into a clearing in the woods. We let the horses have some grass and we ate bread and cheese. Then Rosalind said:

'You had a good sleep. You can stay on the look-out while Petra and I sleep.'

She and Petra lay down and put blankets on top of them. Soon they were asleep.

I sat with my bow and arrows ready. It was very quiet. I could only hear the birds, and the horses eating grass. The sun rose. A few times I walked round the clearing. I found nothing, but it helped me to stay awake.

After about two hours, I could hear Michael.

'Where are you now?' he asked.

I told him. 'We are going to the south-west,' I said. 'We

will ride at night and rest in the day.'

'That's a good plan,' said Michael. 'But there are people everywhere. They are in groups all over the place. They are looking out for Fringes people. If anyone sees the footprints of your big horses the news will spread fast.'

'But I am glad we have got the big horses,' I said. 'They can go for a long way without getting tired.'

'Yes, you will need them,' said Michael. 'But you will need to be very careful too. There are people looking for you everywhere. I am going to join a group. I will say that I have seen you going south-east. Later, Mark will say you have gone north. If anyone sees you, do not let them get away. But do not shoot them. No one is allowed to use guns. If people hear a shot they will know that it is you.'

'I did not bring a gun,' I said. I had not brought a gun because a bow and arrow was much quicker, and made no noise.

Mark spoke. 'I heard what you said,' he said. 'I will be ready to say you have gone north.'

Michael said to me, 'Tell Rosalind to talk to me when she wakes up. Goodbye.'

I stayed on look-out for another two hours. Then I woke Rosalind. I lay down beside Petra and was soon asleep.

26 Sally and Katherine

When I woke up I could see think-pictures from Rosalind. She was talking to Michael and she sounded very upset.

'I have killed him, Michael. He is dead . . .'

Michael said, 'Don't worry, Rosalind, dear. You had to kill him. This is a war now.'

I sat up. 'What has happened?' I asked.

No one answered.

I looked round. Petra was still asleep. The big horses were still eating grass. Michael said:

'Hide him, Rosalind. Put leaves on him.'

I got up. I walked across the clearing. But I did not go far. I did not want to leave Petra alone.

Then Rosalind came out of the bushes. She was cleaning an arrow with some leaves.

'What happened?' I asked again. Rosalind was very upset. She could not talk in think-pictures. She said in words:

'It was a man. He had followed the horses. I saw him . . . Michael said I must kill him . . . Oh, David! I did not want to kill him. But what could I do?'

Her eyes were full of tears. I put my arms round her and let her cry. I told her she was right. She had to kill him.

Later, I went to see if the man had had a horse. I did not find any tracks that a horse could have made. When I got back, Petra was awake. She and Rosalind were talking.

The day went by. Michael did not talk to us. There was nothing to do except wait until dark. So we waited.

Then, in the afternoon, we heard something. It was a call from one of the others. It was not a real think-picture. It was just a cry of pain. It was very loud. Petra cried and ran to Rosalind. My hands shook. We could not tell who was calling.

Then we saw a picture. It was not clear, but it was full of pain. And we knew it was Katherine calling. Rosalind held my hand hard. We waited. Then we heard Sally. She was sending think-pictures of love to Katherine. Then she spoke to us. She was crying and very unhappy.

'They have hurt Katherine,' she said. 'They have hurt her badly. Please, don't be angry with her. They have hurt her so much . . . She had to tell them what she knew. She can't hear us. Oh, Katherine, darling . . .'

Michael spoke.

'It *is* war,' he said. 'Some day I will kill them for hurting Katherine.'

After that there was silence for more than an hour. Rosalind and I tried to calm Petra. She was very frightened and upset.

Then we heard Sally again.

'Katherine has told them everything,' she said. 'I have told them that she told the truth . . .' She stopped, then went on : 'I could not bear the hot irons. I saw what they did to Katherine. I had to tell them. Forgive me, all of you . . . forgive us both.' She stopped again.

Michael spoke. He sounded very upset. He said :

'Sally, dear, we forgive you. Of course we forgive you. We understand. But what have you told them? How much do they know?'

'They know about think-pictures. They know about David and Rosalind,' said Sally.

'Do they know about Petra too?' asked Michael.

'Yes,' said Sally. 'Oh, oh, oh! Poor little Petra. But they knew already. If I had lied they would have known.'

'Do they know about anyone else?' asked Michael.

'No. We have told them that there is no one else. I think they believe it. They are still asking questions. They are trying to understand more about think-pictures,' said Sally. She went on, 'They want to know how we make think-pictures and how far we can send them. I have lied about that. I have told them we can only send them for five miles . . . Katherine is hardly awake. She cannot send think-pictures to you. But they keep on asking questions . . . on and on. If you could see how they have hurt Katherine! Oh Michael, her feet . . . her poor, poor feet.'

Sally was very unhappy. She stopped talking.

No one else spoke. We were all too shocked.

27 Out to Kill . . .

It was nearly dark when Michael spoke again.

'Listen to me,' he told us. 'They are very angry about all this. And they are frightened. There is no way that people can *see* we are different. So they have put up notices. The notices say what you all look like. If anyone helps you to get away they will be punished. Anyone can shoot you now. If anyone catches you alive they will get a lot of money.'

There was silence. Then Rosalind said :

'I don't understand. If we promised to go away and never come back . . .'

'They are afraid of us,' said Michael. 'They want to capture you and learn more about think-pictures. That is why people will be given money if they catch you. They are afraid that there are a lot of us. They think that if there were many of us we could fight them. We could send messages without them knowing. So they are very frightened.'

Rosalind said, 'Are they going to kill Sally and Katherine?'

She stopped quickly. She did not want Sally and Katherine to hear what she had said. We waited. We could hear nothing from Sally and Katherine.

Michael said, 'I do not think they will kill them. They have caught them now. If they killed them it would be different from killing a baby. People have known Sally and Katherine for twenty years. If they were killed, people would be very upset. Now they have caught them that is all they need for the moment.'

'But they can kill *us*?' said Rosalind.

'You are not with people who know you,' said Michael. 'If a stranger sees you he will not mind about killing you.

He will just think you are a Mutant, running away.'

We did not say anything to that. There was nothing we could say. Michael asked:

'Which way are you travelling tonight?'

'Still south-west,' I told him. 'We will have to go into the Fringes, I think.'

'That is a good idea,' said Michael. 'If you hide there for a long time, people may think you are dead. I am going with a group tomorrow. I will say you have gone south-east.'

We stopped talking to Michael. Rosalind put our things on to the horses again. We climbed into the baskets. We started to ride off. Then Petra started to cry.

She said that she did not want to go into the Fringes. She had heard bad stories about the Fringes. She was afraid of Hairy Jack and the monsters who lived there.

It was difficult for us to calm her. We had heard the same bad stories when we were little. And we were frightened too.

Michael spoke again. 'What is the matter?' he said.

We told him. He understood. He started to send think-pictures to Petra. 'You must not be frightened,' he said. 'The people who live in the Fringes are not wicked people. They are unhappy and lonely. Some of them do look strange, but that is not their fault. They are good people inside. What people look like does not matter . . .'

Petra said suddenly: 'Who is the other one talking?'

'What other one? What do you mean?' asked Michael.

'There is someone else making think-pictures,' said Petra.

28   The Woman From Far Away

There was a pause. I opened my mind up. But I could not see any other think-pictures.

'I get nothing,' said Michael. Mark and Rachel said, 'We can't see anything.'

Petra sent a strong think-picture. If she had spoken in words she would have said 'Shut up!' We stopped and waited.

I looked at the other basket. Rosalind had her arm round Petra and was watching her. Petra had her eyes shut tight. We waited.

'What is it?' asked Rosalind.

Petra said, 'Someone is asking questions. She is a very long, long way away I think. She says she has had my afraid-think-pictures before. She wants to know who I am and where I am. Shall I tell her?'

Michael asked us if we thought Petra should tell her. We said yes.

'All right, Petra. Tell her,' he said.

'I shall have to be very loud,' said Petra. We were glad she had told us. I shut my mind. But when Petra sent her think-pictures they were very strong. They were like a flash of very bright light. They made me feel blind and deaf.

Petra stopped for a moment. Michael said: 'Goodness, that was strong!'

'Shut up!' said Petra again. There was another big flash. When it stopped, Michael said:

'Where is the other one?'

'Over there,' said Petra.

'For goodness' sake . . .' said Michael. '*Where?*'

'She is pointing south-west,' I told him.

'Did you ask her the name of the place, darling?' Rosalind asked Petra.

'Yes, but I don't understand it. There are two parts of it and a lot of water,' Petra said in words. 'She does not know where I am, either.'

Rosalind said, 'We will send her letter-shapes. I will give you the letters of Labrador, where we live. Then you send them to her.'

Rosalind made a think-picture of an L. Petra sent it on. Her think-picture was very strong. Then Rosalind gave her an A, then a B until the whole word LABRADOR was sent.

Petra said, 'She understands the word. But she does not know where Labrador is. She says she will find out. She will send us *her* letter-pictures now.'

Petra told us the first letter was a Z. Then she went on: E-A-L-A-N-D.

'ZEALAND,' said Michael. 'That doesn't make sense. Petra must have got the first letter wrong. It must be S, not Z.'

'No!' said Petra. 'It is a Z.'

'But darling,' said Rosalind, 'Zealand doesn't mean anything. If it is Sealand, then of course that means a land in the sea.'

'Wait,' said Petra. She talked to the other person again. We waited.

'It *is* a Z!' said Petra. 'She says it makes a noise like a bee – zzzzz!'

'All right,' said Michael. 'But ask her if there is a lot of sea.'

Petra soon answered. 'Yes, there are two parts of land. And there is sea all around. She says the sun is shining for miles and miles and the sea is all blue . . .'

'In the middle of the night?' asked Michael. 'She must be mad!'

'But it is not night where she is,' said Petra. 'It is a place

78

with a lot of houses. It is quite different from Waknuk. It is much, much bigger. There are funny carts with no horses to pull them. And there are things flying in the air . . .'

I suddenly remembered my dream of the city. I remembered the flying things in the air. I sent Petra a think-picture. It was of a silver thing, with something going round and round on top of it.

'Yes – it is like that,' said Petra.

Michael spoke.

'David! How do you know what the flying thing is like?' he asked.

I stopped him.

'Let's get more about the place from Petra,' I said. 'We can talk about it later.' So once again we tried to close our minds to the think-pictures going to and from Petra and the Zealand woman.

We went slowly through the forest. We had to keep away from the paths so that we did not leave horse-tracks. So we went over rough ground, where the branches of the trees were very low. We had to keep our bows and arrows ready. We did not think we would meet any men, but there were wild animals about. When we saw any animals they ran away. We thought they were frightened because the horses were so big.

The night was short. It was summer and the dark did not last long. Soon we stopped and let the horses eat grass again while we had some food. While we ate, we talked.

Petra told me more about Zealand, the place where the other woman lived. I was very excited. The more she told me, the more it was like my dream. I knew I had not been dreaming about the Old People. I had been dreaming about a place that was in the world now.

But Petra got tired. We stopped talking and she went to sleep. Rosalind went to sleep as well. I stayed on the look-out. In the early morning Michael spoke again. He said:

'They are following you all, David. Do you remember the man whom Rosalind killed? His dog found him afterwards. Then they found the big horse-tracks. They are all moving south-west after you. I am in a group with them. You had better ride on. Go quickly!'

I woke up Rosalind and Petra. In ten minutes we were riding again. This time we rode quite fast. We followed an old path.

Nothing happened for about ten miles. Then we went round a corner. We saw a man riding a horse. He was very close, and he was coming towards us.

29 Our First Fight

The man must have known who we were. He took his bow and arrow and aimed at us at once. We were quicker. We both shot arrows. But they both missed. Then he shot. His arrow went just over our horses' heads. I fired again and missed again. Then Rosalind fired again. Her arrow hit the man's horse. His horse jumped. Then it turned and began to run. I fired again. My arrow hit the horse in a back leg. It jumped to the side and the man fell off. Then the horse ran off very fast.

We did not wait to see the man get up. He pulled himself quickly out of the way as the huge horses ran past him. We rode on as fast as we could. When we looked back we could see the man sitting up. He looked as if he had hurt himself when he fell from his horse. But he did not look badly hurt. We were worried. His horse was in front of us. It had two arrows in it and no rider. When people saw it they would know we were close. Two miles further on the woods stopped. We were facing open fields. On the other side we could see more woods. In the middle of the fields was a small farm. We could see some men and women. The horse with the arrows in it was with them.

There was nothing we could do. So we rode towards them very fast. At first they did not see us. They were looking at the horse. Then they saw us. But our horses were so big that they were frightened. They ran into their houses and the hurt horse galloped off. We rode through the farm at top speed. No one tried to stop us.

The track went to the left, but Rosalind kept her big horse going straight ahead, towards the woods. We kept going faster and faster, leaving a trail of broken fences behind us.

At the edge of the trees, I looked back. The people at the farm had come out from their houses. They were staring at us and making signs for us to stop.

We rode through the woods for about four miles. Then we came to open fields again. We had never seen fields like these before. There were a lot of bushes and the grass was very high. In some places it was nearly ten feet high.

We rode through this strange grass until we came to some trees. They were strange too. But as we rode on we found a clearing. Here the grass looked normal. We thought the horses could eat it. We stopped to rest.

Soon we were eating. We were very hungry. All was quiet. Suddenly we could feel Petra's think-pictures. They were so strong that I bit my tongue. Rosalind put her hand on her head.

'Goodness, Petra!' she said. 'What is happening?'

'Sorry,' said Petra. 'I keep forgetting my think-pictures are so strong.' We waited for her to speak again. Then she said :

'The other one is talking again. She wants to talk to one of you. She says, will you all try to hear her? She will send very strong think-pictures.'

I opened up my mind. But I could see nothing.

'It is no good,' I told Petra. 'You will have to get her think-pictures. Then try to send them to us.'

We waited, while Petra and the other woman talked in think-pictures. My head was full of light and sound, but I could not understand what they were saying. Then Petra made her think-pictures quieter. She tried to tell us what the woman was saying.

It is hard to say what she told us. But the other woman said that Petra was very important. She was very clever to send think-pictures as strong as hers. The woman would try to send help to us. Until then we must keep Petra safe, no matter what happened.

'Did you understand that?' I asked Michael.

'Yes!' he said. 'But there is something very strange. That woman said that she was surprised that we could talk in think-pictures. She thinks that we are very simple people. She cannot understand how simple people can talk like that. She cannot understand how Petra can send such strong think-pictures.'

'But we are not simple people!' I said. 'Perhaps Petra did not tell her who we were. Perhaps this woman thinks we are Fringes people.'

'No!' said Petra strongly. 'I did not tell her we are Fringes people!'

'Well, it is very strange,' I said. 'And I don't understand how this woman can send help to us. She is south-west. Everyone knows there are miles and miles of Badlands there. Even if she is on the other side of them, how can she come to us?'

Rosalind said, 'Let's wait and see what happens. I am too tired to go on talking now.'

I was tired too. We told Petra to keep watch. She had slept for a long time in the basket. Then Rosalind and I lay down. We were soon asleep.

30 We are Attacked

When I woke up it was nearly dark. Petra was shaking my arm. 'Michael wants to talk to you,' she said. I cleared my mind for him. He said :

'They are following you again. The people on that little farm said they had seen you. There is a big group of people on the farm there now. They are getting ready to follow you. If you leave now you should have time to get away.'

'All right,' I said. I was very tired. Then I asked Michael : 'What happened to Sally and Katherine?'

'I don't know,' said Michael. 'I can't get an answer from them. Does any one know?'

Rachel spoke. Her think-pictures were faint because she was a long way away now.

'Katherine is still asleep. I can't get any answer. Mark and I are afraid . . .' said Rachel.

'Go on,' said Michael.

'Well, Katherine has been asleep for a very long time. We think perhaps – perhaps she is dead,' said Rachel.

'And what about Sally?' asked Michael.

Rachel did not say anything for a few minutes. Then she said :

'We think – we are afraid something is wrong with Sally's mind. We cannot understand anything she says. And her think-pictures are very faint.'

Rachel sounded very unhappy.

Michael spoke. He sounded very hard, and very angry.

'Do you understand what that means, David? They are really afraid of us. Once they have caught us they will hurt us. They will try to find out how our minds work. You must not let them catch Rosalind and Petra. It would be better to kill them. You understand?'

I looked at Rosalind. She was still asleep. She looked very pretty. I thought about Katherine, and how they had hurt her. I thought about them hurting Rosalind and Petra. I felt very afraid and unhappy.

But I knew it would be better to kill them than let them be caught. I could hear Rachel and Michael sending me think-pictures. They were telling me not to worry. Then they stopped.

I looked at Petra. She was looking at me. She had seen our think-pictures. She did not look frightened. She looked rather surprised. She said :

'Why did Michael say you must kill Rosalind and me?'

'I must only kill you if they catch us,' I said. I tried to sound as if that was normal. Petra thought about it.

'Why?' she asked.

'Well,' I said, 'you see, we are different from other people. They cannot make think-pictures. They are afraid of us . . .'

'But why are they afraid? We are not hurting them,' said Petra.

'I don't know why they are afraid,' I said. 'But they are. They just feel afraid. They think everyone should be the same. And when they are afraid they get cruel and wicked.'

Petra did not understand.

'It is difficult to understand,' I said. 'But the main thing is this : we don't want you and Rosalind to be hurt. Do you remember when you got hot water on your foot? Do you remember how it hurt? Well, if they catch us they will hurt us much more than that. It is much better to be dead than to be hurt like that.'

I looked down at Rosalind. She looked so pretty. I kissed her. She didn't wake up.

Later, Petra said :

'David, when you kill Rosalind and me . . .'

I put my arm round her. 'It won't happen, darling,' I said. 'I will only kill you if they catch us. And we won't let them catch us. Now, let's wake up Rosalind. But we won't tell her what we have been talking about. She would be worried. So let's keep it a secret. All right?'

'All right,' said Petra.

We woke up Rosalind. Then we had some food, and waited for it to get dark. Petra was very quiet while we ate. Then she said:

'Zealand must be a funny place. Everyone there can make think-pictures. Well, nearly everyone. And no one wants to hurt people who make think-pictures.'

'Oh,' said Rosalind, 'Have you been talking to the other woman again?'

'Yes,' said Petra. 'She says that most people there can't make very good think-pictures though. They make them like you and David.'

'Well, thank you!' said Rosalind.

Petra went on, 'But *she* is very good at it. And she has two babies. She says when they grow up they will make very good think-pictures too. But she says I make stronger think-pictures than anyone! She says when I grow up I must have babies. Then I can teach them to make strong think-pictures too. She says I can make stronger think-pictures than anyone at all.'

'Well!' said Rosalind. 'It seems to me that making think-pictures is very dangerous.'

'But it is not dangerous *there*,' said Petra. 'She says everyone *wants* to make think-pictures in Zealand. People who can't do them work very hard to try to do them.'

I thought about what Uncle Axel had told me. I remembered him telling me about the places further away than the Black Coasts. He had said that everyone thought that *they* were the true image and that everyone else was a Mutant.

When there were stars in the sky we set off again. We went quietly through the woods. We rode for miles and miles. We could hear nothing but the slow footsteps of the horses.

After about three hours we saw that it was very dark in

85

front of us. We could just see the edge of more woods. There were a lot of trees, very close together. We thought we would ride on towards the trees and see if we could get through them.

We had got very near the trees when suddenly we heard a gun go off. The bullet flew past us.

Both our horses were shocked. I nearly fell out of my basket. The horses jumped into the air. Then the rope that kept them together broke. The horse who had been behind us ran off towards the woods. Then he ran to the left. The horse we had been riding ran after it.

We could not do anything except stay in the baskets. The horse ran and ran, kicking up the earth. We heard another shot. The horse went even faster . . .

Then there was another shot in front of us. The horse turned and ran into the woods. We hid even lower in the baskets. We went into the woods where the trees were not very close together. But it was still a very frightening ride. The horse had to go more slowly because of the trees. I did not dare to look out of the basket because the branches were so low. But I did not think anyone could be following us. If a normal-size horse had tried to follow it would have been torn open by the snapped-off branches we left behind.

At last our horse grew calm. It slowed down and went carefully through the trees and branches. The trees grew thinner. After a time we could see stars. We came to a path, and rode down it. Suddenly we heard a noise. We quickly picked up our bows and arrows. But it was only the other horse. He was glad to see us. He started to follow us again. The path went past rocks and streams, and through thick trees.

We thought we must be in the Fringes by now. We did not know if the Waknuk people would still try to follow us. We did not know if we should keep the two big horses. If the Waknuk people *were* following us, and getting close, it would be better to leave the horses. We could send them off on another track, and the Waknuk people would follow that. But if the Waknuk people were nowhere near us, it would be silly to leave the horses and walk. We were very tired.

We tried to talk to Michael, to ask him what was happening. But he did not answer, and we thought he must be asleep.

So we rode on. We went on to a path where the trees were very thick. The branches met above us so we could not see the stars. It was very dark.

Suddenly, something fell on me. It was very quick – I could not use my bow and arrow. My breath was knocked out of my body. I felt something hit me on the head. Then everything went black.

31 Going to the Fringes

Slowly, slowly, I began to see again. Rosalind was calling me. It was the real Rosalind, the one whom I hardly ever saw. For so long she had kept her real self hidden, and shown me – and everyone else – only a cold, down-to-earth Rosalind.

I loved the girl I could see. I loved her tall slim shape, her small pointed breasts and long legs. I loved her golden hair and the way she moved. All these were easy to love, without knowing the real person underneath.

But now, the under-Rosalind was calling to me, gently, sadly. My love went out to her, and hers came back to me. We loved each other so much that it seemed as if we were one person.

Then we were apart again. I saw that the sky was grey. My body hurt. Then I could hear Michael. He sounded worried.

'What happened?' he asked.

'I don't know – something hit me,' I told him. 'I think I am all right now. But my head aches and I can't move properly.'

As I said that I saw why I could not move. I was still in the basket. I had been pushed right down inside it. The horse was still moving.

Michael asked Rosalind what had happened.

'Some Fringes people jumped down on us from the branches. There were four or five of them. One landed right on top of David,' she said. 'Now I am in one basket on the first horse. My hands are tied together. David is in a basket on the horse behind.'

'And where is Petra?' asked Michael quickly.

'Oh, she is all right,' said Rosalind. 'She is in the other basket on this horse. She is talking to the man in charge.'

'And you are going right into the Fringes?' asked Michael.

'Yes,' said Rosalind.

'Well, that is perhaps the best thing,' said Michael. 'Are the Fringes people going to hurt you?'

'I don't think so,' said Rosalind. 'They just don't want to let us get away. They don't know who we are. I think they care more about the big horses than about us.'

'And you don't know what they are going to do with you?' asked Michael.

'No. I asked the man on this horse where we were going, but I don't think he knows.'

'Well . . .' said Michael. For once he did not seem to know what to say. 'Well, there are a lot of people with me now. They are planning to come into the Fringes to follow you. But they don't want to come in small groups. So there will be a lot of us coming together. I don't know what you can do now. I think we will just have to wait and see what happens.'

Then he said goodbye.

I moved in my basket. Slowly I stood up. There was a man in the other basket. He looked at me. He looked quite friendly.

'Stop now!' he called to the horse. The horse slowed down and stopped. The man gave me some water from a bottle. Then we went on. Now I was standing up, I could see where we were going. My father had been right about the Fringes – there was nothing normal here. The trees looked very strange. Some of them had trunks that were so soft that the trees could not stand up, but grew along the ground. I saw some rocks. As we got close to them I saw that they were not rocks at all. They were very big mushrooms. In other places there were tiny trees that looked very old.

I looked again at the man in the other basket. I could not see anything wrong with him. He was just very dirty. He saw me look at him.

'Have you never been in the Fringes before, boy?' he asked.

'No,' I told him. 'Is it all like this?'

He smiled and shook his head.

'Every part of the Fringes is different,' he said. 'Nothing is in the true image yet.'

'Yet?' I asked. 'Do you think things will get like the true image one day?'

'Of course,' the man said. 'It takes a long time. But where you have come from was Fringes once. It looks as though God is having a game. But he is taking a long time.'

'God?' I said. 'I thought that the Devil was in the Fringes. God lives where we come from.'

'That is what you have been told,' he said. 'But it is not true. Where you live, people think they are always right. They think they live like the Old People. They think every plant and animal there is in the true image. Or they try to get rid of Mutants and Offences. But one day God will teach them a lesson. He will show them that they are not always right.'

'Oh,' I said. I did not know what to say.

The man waved his hand at the land around us. Suddenly I saw what was wrong with him. On his right hand he had only two fingers.

'Look at all this,' he said. 'One day good things will grow here. Out of all this, new life will grow. Your people cannot understand that. They think that all change is wrong. Your people are wicked to think that.'

I did not really understand what the man was saying. So I asked him why we had been caught. He did not really know. But he said that people who came into the Fringes were always caught. I thought about that. Then I talked to Michael.

'What shall we tell the Fringes people?' I asked. 'They will want to know why we are running away. They will not see what is wrong with us.'

'Tell them the truth,' said Michael. 'But only tell them a little. Just tell them enough so that they can understand what we can do.'

'All right,' I said. 'Do you understand that, Petra? You tell the Fringes people that you can make think-pictures. But just tell them you can talk like that to Rosalind and me. Don't tell them about Michael, or the Zealand people.'

Petra said, 'The Zealand people are coming to help us. They are not so far away now.'

Michael did not believe her. 'I *hope* they are coming,' he said. 'But I do not see how they can. Anyway, do not say anything about them to the Fringes people.'

'All right,' said Petra.

Rosalind and I told the Fringes men that people from Waknuk were following us. The men did not seem surprised.

'Good,' said one of them. We rode on.

32 Talking to the Zealand Woman

Petra started to talk to the woman in Zealand again. Rosalind and I knew that the woman was not so far away. Petra's think-pictures were not so strong. For the first time I could understand a little of what the woman said. So could Rosalind. She made think-pictures as strong as she could. She found that she and the woman could talk to each other.

Rosalind told the woman where we were. 'I do not think we are in danger at the moment,' said Rosalind.

The woman said: 'Be careful. Tell the Fringes people that you are in danger from your own people. They may not trust you because you look like Norms. Tell them that you are very different from Norms *inside*. Whatever happens, look after the little girl. We have never known someone so young who could make such strong think-pictures. What is her name?'

Rosalind made letter-pictures: P-E-T-R-A. Then she asked the woman:

'But who are you? What is Zealand?'

'We are the New People,' said the woman. 'We are your kind of people. We can send think-pictures and we are going to make a new world. The new world will be different from the Old People's world. It will be a much better place. You have been told that the Old People were good. That is not true. And most of them could only talk with words. We are much better than they were.'

Rosalind asked her: 'Where do you come from? How can so many of you send think-pictures?'

'You know about the Tribulation, don't you?' asked the woman.

'Yes,' said Rosalind. 'It was like a big earthquake and all the Old People died.'

'That is right,' said the woman. 'Well, even in the time of the Old People, there were some who could make think-pictures. They lived on two islands. When the Tribulation came, some of them were killed, but not all. Slowly, more people were born who could make think-pictures. They married each other when they grew up. And so after a time there were very many of them.

'That is how we began,' the woman went on. 'We stayed on these two islands, called Zealand. We know that there are some places, like Labrador, where you live, where people think it is wrong to make think-pictures. So we try to help people like you. But we have never talked to people so far away before. It is because of Petra that we heard about you. You must look after her. It is difficult for me to talk to you. You are such a long way away. I must stop now. I will try to help you soon. Look after Petra.'

The woman stopped talking.

I said to Michael :

'Did you hear all that ?'

'Yes,' he said. 'But I still do not understand how she can come to help us. We are all coming after you now. We shall soon be in the Fringes.'

We rode slowly on. The land was still full of strange plants and trees. It felt good when we got to some open country. We stopped only once for food and drink. Then we rode on. We went through more woods, until we got to a river. We rode along the bank for a time.

Then we got to a place where there was a big tree. It was a strange shape, like a pear. Below it was a path down the bank to the river. We rode down it and then the horses went across the river, through the water.

There were cliffs on the other side. There was a very narrow path through the cliffs. We rode through it. It was so narrow that the baskets touched the sides. Then it got wider and at last we came to the end of it. We had come right through the cliffs and were now on the other side of the river.

Seven or eight men were standing there. They had bows and arrows in their hands.

33 The Spider-Man Again

The men there looked hard at the big horses. They looked frightened because the horses were so big. When we reached them we stopped.

The man in the other basket said to me :

'Down you get, boy.'

Petra and Rosalind were climbing down from the other big horse. The man gave the horses a push and they went on. Petra took my hand. She was frightened. But the men were more interested in the horses than us. We looked at the men.

There was nothing really frightening about them. One of them had six fingers on one hand. Another had no hair on his head at all. Another had very big feet and hands.

None of them looked like a monster. We all felt better. When the men had seen the horses go away, they turned to us. Two of them said that we must go with them. The rest of the men stayed where they were.

We went with the two men down a path through some woods. Then we got to a clearing. On the right of the clearing was a wall of cliffs. All the way up the cliffs were holes. There were ladders made of branches going up to the holes.

On the ground in front were some rough huts and tents.

There were one or two fires. A few men and quite a lot of women were there. They did not seem to be doing much.

We walked through the huts and tents until we came to the biggest. It was made of wooden poles, with the cover from a cart on top. A man was sitting on a stool in front of the tent. He looked up as we went over.

For a moment I got a shock. The man looked just like my father. Then I knew that I had seen him before. He was the 'spider-man' who had been caught about eight years ago. I had seen him in the yard of the farm at Waknuk.

The two men with us pushed us towards the spider-man. He looked at the three of us. I did not like the way he looked at Rosalind. She did not like that look either. Then he looked carefully at me. He nodded.

'Do you remember me?' he said.

'Yes,' I told him.

He looked away from me. Then he looked all round the huts and tents. He looked back at me.

'This is not much like Waknuk,' he said.

'Not much,' I said.

He was silent for some time. Then he said:

'Do you know who I am?'

'I think so,' I said. 'I think I found out.'

'Well?' he said. 'Who am I?'

I said:

'My father had an older brother. His family thought the brother was a Norm. Then, when he was three years old, they knew he was a Mutant. His legs and arms were much too long. He was taken into the Fringes.'

'Yes,' said the spider-man, 'I am that man. I am older than your father. Waknuk should be mine. It would be mine – except for *this*.'

He put out a long arm and looked at it. Then he dropped it. He looked at me again.

'Do you know how long a man's arm should be?' he asked me.

94

'No,' I said.

'Nor do I,' said the man. 'But some inspector does. So, because my arms and legs are too long, I cannot live at Waknuk. I must live like a wild man, with other wild men.'

He stopped, then he asked me:

'Are you the oldest son?'

'I am the only son,' I said. 'There was a younger brother, but . . .'

'But he was a Mutant?' asked the man. 'I see. And now you have lost Waknuk!'

I thought about that. I did not think I had ever wanted to own Waknuk. I had always known, somehow, that people would find out I could make think-pictures. I had always know that Waknuk would never be mine. I said to the man:

'I do not mind about losing Waknuk. I am glad to be away from it. I am glad to be safe.'

The man did not like that.

'You are not very brave,' he said. 'Don't you want to fight to get Waknuk? It should be yours.'

'It should be *yours*,' I told him. 'But I mean that I am glad I don't have to go on hiding.'

'We are all hiding here,' said the spider-man.

'Perhaps you are,' I said. 'But you can be yourselves here. You don't have to pretend that you are Norms. You don't have to think before you speak.'

The man nodded.

'We heard about you all,' he said. 'We know that you can make think-pictures. We have ways of finding things out. But I do not understand why so many people are trying to catch you.'

'We think that they are frightened of us,' I said. 'We have lived with them so long, and they never knew we could make think-pictures. They think there may be many more of us. So they want to catch us and make us tell them.'

95

I could hear Michael and Rosalind talking. But I could not talk in words and in think-pictures at the same time. So I did not listen to them.

The man said:

'So they are coming after you into the Fringes? Do you know how many of them are coming?'

'I am not sure,' I said. I did not know what to tell him.

'Well, you should be able to find out,' said the man.

I wondered if the spider-man knew about Michael. He went on:

'Do not lie to us, boy. It is you they are after. If they come here it will make trouble for us. Why should we care what happens to you? It would be easy for us to leave you where they can find you.'

Petra understood what he meant. She said quickly:

'More than a hundred men are coming.'

He looked at her for a moment. Then he said:

'So there *is* one of you with them. Someone is sending you think-pictures. I thought there was,' he said.

'A hundred men is a lot of people to send after you three. Too many ... I see ...'

He turned back to me. He said:

'Have there been stories about trouble in the Fringes? Did you hear stories before you ran away?'

'Yes,' I said.

'I see,' he said. 'They will come to catch you. And they will fight us at the same time. How near are they now?'

I asked Michael. He said they still had quite a long way to come.

'Is your father with them?' asked the man.

I did not want to ask Michael that.

'No,' I said.

'That is a pity,' said the spider-man. 'I have wanted to see him again for a long time. Perhaps your father is not as keen to catch Mutants as I thought.' He looked at me hard.

Then, quite suddenly, he turned to look at Rosalind. He

looked at her hard for a long time. Rosalind looked back at him, very coldly. Then, suddenly she looked away. She went red. The man smiled.

The man thought he had beaten Rosalind. He thought she would do what he asked. But he was wrong. Rosalind had not given in to him. She was very frightened. She felt like a child, looking at a monster.

Petra knew how Rosalind felt, and she screamed.

I jumped at the man. He fell off his stool and I hit him hard. Then the two men who had come with us pulled me away.

The spider-man sat up and rubbed his face. He smiled at me, but it was a cold smile. He said :

'That was brave, boy. But it will not do any good.' He got up on his long legs. 'You have not seen many of the women in the Fringes, have you? Perhaps when you see them you will understand things better. This girl can have children. I have wanted some children for a long time. I do not mind if they look like me.'

He smiled again, then he looked angry.

'You had better face it, boy,' he said. 'I do not give second chances.'

He turned to the two men.

'Take him out of the Fringes,' he said. 'And if he does not stay out, shoot him.'

The two men pulled me round and took me away. At the end of the clearing, one of the men kicked me.

'Keep on going,' he said.

I turned round, but one of them had his bow and arrow ready. So I kept going. I went a little way into the trees. Then I crept back under some bushes.

They knew I would do that. But they did not shoot me. They beat me up and threw me back to the bushes. I remember flying through the air. But I don't remember coming down . . .

34 The Girl in the Fringes

I was being pulled along. Someone was holding my arms. My face was hit by branches as I was pulled.

A voice behind me said: 'Sssh!'

'Give me a minute. I will be all right,' I said.

The pulling stopped. I lay for a few moments and then sat up. A young woman was sitting looking at me.

The sun was low now. There was not much light in the trees. I could not see the young woman well. I saw dark hair and a brown face. I could see bright dark eyes looking at me. The young woman's dress was dirty and torn. But what I noticed most was that there was no cross on her dress. I had never seen a woman before who did not have a cross on her dress. It looked very strange. We looked at each other for a few seconds. Then she said sadly:

'You don't know who I am, David.'

Until she spoke I had not known who she was. But when she said 'David' like that, I knew.

'Sophie!' I said. 'Oh, Sophie . . . !'

She smiled.

'Dear David,' she said. 'Have they hurt you badly?'

I tried moving my arms and legs. They hurt. So did my body and my head.

I felt dry blood on my face. But nothing was broken. I started to get up. Sophie put a hand on my arm.

'Not yet,' she said. 'Wait until it is dark.' She went on looking at me. 'I saw them bring you into the Fringes,' she said. 'You and the little girl – and the other girl. Who is she, David?'

That made me think suddenly of Rosalind and Petra. I tried to send think-pictures to them, but there was no answer. I felt very worried. Then Michael came in. He sounded glad to hear me.

'Thank goodness you are all right,' he said. 'We have been very worried about you. Take it easy now. Rosalind and Petra are very tired. They are asleep.'

'Is Rosalind . . .?' I could not ask the whole question.

'She is all right, I tell you,' he said. 'What has been happening to you?'

I told him. We only talked for a few moments. But when we stopped I saw Sophie looking at me.

'Who is that other girl, David?' she asked again.

I said that Rosalind was my cousin. She looked at me as I spoke. Then she nodded slowly.

'He wants her, doesn't he?' she said. She meant the spider-man.

'That is what he said,' I said.

'Could Rosalind give him babies?' Sophie went on.

'I do not want to talk about it,' I said.

'So you are in love with her?' Sophie said.

'We love each other,' I said.

Sophie nodded. She picked up a few twigs and broke them. Then she said: 'He has gone away. He is where the fighting is. She is safe just now.'

'She is asleep,' I told her. 'Petra is asleep too.'

She looked into my eyes.

'How do you know?' she said.

I tried to tell her about think-pictures. I told her as simply as I could. She went on breaking twigs while I spoke. Then she nodded.

'I remember,' she said. 'My mother said there was something . . . something about you. She said you seemed to understand her before she spoke. Was that it?'

'I think so,' I said. 'I think your mother could send think-pictures too. But she did not know she could.'

'It must be a wonderful thing to do,' said Sophie. 'It is like having more eyes, inside you.'

'Something like that,' I said. 'It is hard to explain. But it isn't all wonderful. It can hurt a lot sometimes.'

'If you are any kind of Mutant, you are hurt – always,' said Sophie.

She sat there and looked ahead. She was thinking.

At last she said :

'If Rosalind can give him babies, he won't want me any more.'

There was enough light for me to see tears on her face.

'Sophie dear,' I said. 'Are you in love with him – this spider-man?'

'Oh, don't call him that, please,' said Sophie. 'We cannot help being what we are. His name is Gordon. He is kind to me. He likes me. You cannot understand how much that means. You cannot understand how lonely I get here. I would have given him babies if I could. But you know what people do to stop us having babies. Oh! Why do they do that to us? Why didn't they kill me? It would have been kinder than this . . .'

She sat still. She made no sound, but the tears ran down her face. I took her hand.

I thought about the last time I had seen her. I had stood and waved goodbye as she and her mother and father rode into the trees. I had held a piece of her hair and a yellow ribbon in my hand. I looked at Sophie now and my heart hurt.

'Sophie,' I said, 'Sophie, darling. It will not happen. Rosalind will never let it happen. Do you understand? I *know* that.'

She opened her eyes again. They were full of tears.

'You cannot *know* something like that about someone else. You are just saying that,' she said.

'I'm not, Sophie, I do know. You and I can only know a little about each other. But with Rosalind it is different. When you can make think-pictures with someone, you know everything about them,' I said.

'Is that really true?' asked Sophie. 'I don't understand...'

'How can you understand?' I said. 'But it *is* true. I know what Rosalind thinks about that spider . . . about that man.'

'Can you see what I think?' asked Sophie.

'No more than you can see what I think,' I told her. 'It is just that we can talk all our thoughts if we like. If we do not want to, we don't make think-pictures.'

It was hard to tell Sophie about it. I went on trying, but then I saw that all the light had gone. I could not see her. I stopped.

'Is it dark enough now?' I said.

'Yes,' she said. 'We can go now. Can you walk all right? It isn't far.'

35   The Cave in the Cliffs

I got up. My whole body hurt. but there was nothing badly wrong with me. Sophie could see better in the dark than I could. She took my hand and led the way.

We stayed in the trees, but I could see the light from fires on my left. I knew that we were going round the camp. We went on until we came to the wall of cliffs. We walked some way under the cliffs. Then Sophie stopped. She put my hand on one of the wood ladders against the cliff. 'Follow me,' she said quietly. Then she climbed up the ladder quickly.

I climbed up the ladder more slowly. I got to the top. The ladder stopped by a piece of rock that stuck out from the side of the cliff. There was a hole above the rock. Sophie put her arm out of the hole in the cliff. She helped me get into the hole.

'Sit down,' she told me. She moved about, looking for something. She found a flint, a stone for making fire. She hit it with a bit of steel and sparks flew out. She lit two candles. They were short and fat and they smelt very bad, but now I could see where I was.

It was a cave, about fifteen feet long and nine feet wide. It was cut out of the cliff-rock. It had no door, but there was an animal skin hung at the front. Water dripped slowly from the roof. It fell into a bucket. The bucket was full and the water ran all the way down the cave. In one corner was a bed made of branches. It had skins on it. There were a few black bowls and spoons. There were a few knives on the wall. There was a spear and a bow and arrows by the mattress. There was nothing else.

Sophie found a piece of rag. She put it in the bucket and came over to me. She washed the blood off my face and out of my hair. She looked at my head.

'It is just a cut. It isn't deep,' she said.

I washed my hands.

'Are you hungry, David?' she asked.

'Very hungry,' I told her. I had hardly eaten all day.

'Stay here,' she said. 'I won't be long.' She went out of the cave and down the ladder.

I looked at the shadows on the walls and listened to the drip of the water. I thought about Sophie's old home, with her mother and father. It had been very clean and light. I looked round the cave again. I thought: in the Fringes, perhaps they think this is a good place to live. I felt lonely, and sent think-pictures to Michael.

'Where are you? What has been happening?' I asked him.

'We have stopped for the night,' he said. 'It is too dangerous to go on in the dark. It has been a hard day. These Fringes people know the woods well. Some of them have attacked us from the trees. Three of our men have been killed. Seven men have been hurt.'

'But you are still coming on?' I asked.

'Yes,' said Michael. 'People think that now there are so many of us we can give the Fringes people a good beating. And they want to catch you three. There is a story that there are a lot of us who can make think-pictures. They want to catch you so that you can say who the others are.'

He stopped talking for a moment. When he spoke again he sounded unhappy. 'You know, David,' he said. 'I think there is only one of the others left.'

'*One?*' I said.

'I can hardly talk to Rachel now,' said Michael. 'She is so far away now. But she says something has happened to Mark.'

'Have they caught him?' I asked.

'No. She does not think they have. He would have told her if he had been caught. He just stopped sending think-pictures very suddenly. She hasn't heard from him for over twenty-four hours.'

'Perhaps he has had an accident,' I said. 'Do you remember Walter, the boy who was killed by a tree? He just stopped like that.'

'It might be an accident. Rachel just does not know. She is frightened. She is all alone now. When I have come further into the Fringes I won't be able to talk to her. It will be too far away'.

'But when Petra wakes up she can talk to Rachel,' I said.

'Oh yes,' said Michael. 'I forgot that.'

A few moments later Sophie came into the cave with a bowl of food. It was strange food: little plants, meat cut up, and hard bread. But it was all right. I had nearly finished when I had a very bright flash in my head. The rest of the food fell down my shirt. Petra was awake again. She was very unhappy.

I answered her at once, and she sounded very pleased. But her think-pictures were still very strong. She woke up

Rosalind. I could hear Rosalind, and Michael and the Zealand woman all at once.

Soon Petra became calm. Michael said :

'What the hell was that about?'

Petra said, 'We thought David was dead. We thought they had killed him.'

Now I began to see Rosalind's think-pictures. At first they were not clear, then they became firm. They were full of love and happiness. I felt sad and happy at the same time. For a few moments we spoke only to each other. It was Michael who put an end to that.

'Come on, you two,' he said. 'This is hardly fair on other people! We have important things to talk about. Now, what is happening?'

36   Escape from the Spider-Man

Rosalind said that she and Petra were still in the spider-man's tent. He had gone away. A man was watching them. He was very big, with white hair and pink eyes.

I told the others that I was in the cave with Sophie.

'Right,' said Michael. 'Now, David: do you think this spider-man is going to fight us? Or do you think he will go back to the tent soon?'

'I have no idea,' I told him.

Rosalind came in. She sounded very unhappy and she said :

'I am frightened of the spider-man. He is like an animal. If he tries to make love to me I shall kill myself . . .'

'You won't do anything so damn silly,' said Michael. 'If

the spider-man comes after you, you must kill him.' Then he spoke as loud as he could to the Zealand woman. He said :

'Do you think you can come to help us soon?'

When she spoke we knew she was still a long way away. But we could easily hear her now.

'Yes,' she said calmly.

'When?' Michael asked.

There was silence for a moment. Then the woman said : 'In not more than sixteen hours from now.'

Michael said, 'Then we must somehow keep you three safe until then.'

'Wait a minute. Just hold on a bit,' I told them.

I looked up at Sophie. In the smoky light of the candles I saw her watching me closely. She said :

'Were you "talking" to Rosalind?'

'Yes. And I was talking to Petra, my sister, as well,' I said. 'They are awake now. They are in the tent. A man is watching them. Do you think we can get them out before the spider – before that man comes back? I think we must do it now. Once he does come back . . .'

Sophie turned her head away and looked at the candles. Then she nodded.

'Yes,' she said. 'That will be best for all of us – all of us except him.' She sounded sad. 'Yes, I think it can be done.'

'Now?' I asked.

She nodded again. I picked up the spear that lay by the bed. She looked at it and shook her head.

'You must stay here, David,' she told me.

'But . . .' I began.

'No. If anyone saw you they would kill you. I often go to his tent. If I go no one will take any notice.'

I knew she was right. I put the spear down, but I was worried.

'But can you . . .' I began.

'Yes,' said Sophie.

She got up. She took a knife off the wall of the cave. It was very sharp and bright. She put it in the belt of her skirt. Then she turned and looked at me for a long moment.

'David – ' she said.

'What?' I asked.

Sophie said:

'Tell Rosalind and Petra they must not make any noise. Whatever happens, they must be very, very quiet. Tell them to follow me. Tell them to put dark bits of cloth round themselves. Will you tell them all that?'

'Yes,' I said. 'But I wish you would let me go . . .'

'No,' she said. 'It would be too dangerous. You do not know the place.'

She put out the candles. She went past the skin at the front of the cave. Then she was gone.

I told Rosalind what she had said. We both told Petra she must be very quiet. Then there was nothing more I could do. I sat in the dark, listening to the drip-drip of the water from the roof.

I could not sit still like that for long. I went to the front of the cave and looked out. I could see a few fires. People were moving about quietly. I could hear voices. I heard the cry of a night bird. Nothing more.

We were all waiting. Then, from Rosalind, came a think-picture. She just said, 'It is all right,' but she sounded shocked.

I listened. There was no more noise outside. I waited a long time. Then I heard a noise on the ladder. I moved back into the cave.

Then Rosalind said:

'Is this the right place? Are you there, David?'

'Yes. Come along up,' I said.

One shape came into the front of the cave. Then another, smaller one. Then a third. The candles were lit again.

Then we watched Sophie wash the blood off her arms and off the knife.

37　Rosalind and Sophie

Rosalind and Sophie looked at each other. Sophie looked at Rosalind's dress. It was brown wool, with the cross sewn on to it. Sophie looked at her own dirty, torn skirt. She saw blood on her shirt, took it off and put it in the water. She said to Rosalind:

'You must get rid of that cross. Petra too. It marks you. In the Fringes, we women do not feel that the cross helped us. And the men do not like it. Here.'

She took a small knife from the wall and gave it to Rosalind. Rosalind looked at it and then down at the cross. She had never worn a dress with no cross on it. Sophie watched her.

'I used to wear a cross,' she said. 'It did not help me much.'

Rosalind looked at me. I nodded.

'Sophie is right. It would be dangerous for you to wear a cross in the Fringes,' I said.

Rosalind took the knife and began to pick at the stitches. I said to Sophie:

'What now? Shall we try to get away before it is light?'

'No,' said Sophie. 'They may find that dead man any time. When they do, they will think that you killed him. They will think all three of you are in the wools. They will go to find you. But they will never think of looking here.'

'Do you mean we stay here?' I asked. She nodded.

'For two or three days,' she said. 'When they have stopped looking for you I will help you to get away.'

Rosalind looked up. She stopped picking at the stitches on her cross. 'Why are you doing all this for us?' she asked Sophie.

I talked to her in think-pictures. I told her that Sophie

loved the spider-man. She did not want Rosalind to give him babies.

Sophie and Rosalind looked at each other. Sophie stopped washing her shirt. She stood up. She bent down over Rosalind. Her dark hair hung down on her naked breasts.

'Damn you,' she said angrily. 'Leave me alone, damn you!'

Rosalind went stiff. I moved, ready to jump between them. For long seconds the two girls looked at each other. Sophie was dirty, half-naked, ready to attack. Rosalind looked very pretty in her brown dress, with the cross half-off. Her hair shone in the candle-light.

Then Sophie looked less angry. She did not move away. She stood there, shaking, and watching Rosalind. Then she said again:

'Damn you! Go on, laugh at me. Damn your pretty face. Laugh at me because I *do* want him!' She gave a strange, sad laugh. 'And what is the point in me loving him? What good am I to him? I can never give him babies – never!'

She put her hands on her face, and stood shaking. Then she turned and threw herself on the bed. She began to cry.

We all looked at her, as she lay there in the shadows. One of her shoes had fallen off. I could see her dirty foot, and her six toes. I turned to Rosalind. She looked very upset. She started to get up. I shook my head and she sat down again.

The only sounds in the cave were Sophie crying and the drip-drip-drip of the water.

Petra looked at us, then at Sophie on the bed, then at us again. Then she went over to the bed. She put her hand on Sophie's dark hair.

'Don't cry,' said Petra. '*Please* don't.'

The crying stopped for a moment. Then Sophie put an arm round Petra. The crying got quieter. It was not so sad. But it still made my heart hurt ...

At last I went to sleep.

38   Rachel is Afraid

When I woke up, I was stiff and cold. I had been lying on the hard rock floor. Michael spoke at once:

'Are you going to sleep all day?' he asked.

I looked up, I saw light from under the skin at the front of the cave.

'What is the time?' I asked.

'About eight o'clock,' said Michael. 'It has been light for three hours. We have fought a battle already.'

'What happened?' I asked.

'We knew there were a few Fringes men watching us,' said Michael. 'So we sent some men to catch them. But there were more Fringes men behind the trees. There was a fight. Three of our men are hurt. But there are a lot of us. The Fringes men have run away.'

'So are you coming on now?' I asked.

'Yes. I think the Fringes men will get together again. But at the moment there is nothing to stop us.'

This was bad news. I told Michael that we could not come out of the cave. But if the Waknuk men came and won a battle with the Fringes men, they would look for us. They would find us in the cave.

'What about the Zealand woman?' asked Michael. 'Do you really think she will bring help?'

The Zealand woman spoke. She said:

'We *are* coming to help.'

'How long will you be now?' asked Michael.

'About eight and a half hours from now,' said the Zealand woman. Then she said:

'We are coming over Badlands now. It is a terrible place. I have never seen any place so bad. Everything is black. The ground is like black glass. There are black mountains.

It is like going over hell . . . it is very frightening. If we were not coming to help you, we would go back . . .'

Petra heard that. She sent a very strong think-picture. She was very unhappy. She did not want the Zealand woman to go back. I went to calm her and then the Zealand woman talked to her. She told Petra that she was coming to help us.

Then Michael said :

'David, what about Rachel?'

I said to Petra :

'Petra, darling, we are too far away to talk to Rachel. Will you ask her something,'

Petra nodded. I said :

'Ask Rachel if she has heard anything from Mark.'

Petra asked Rachel. Then she shook her head.

'No,' Petra said. 'Rachel has not heard anything from Mark. She is very unhappy, I think. She wants to know if Michael is all right.'

'Tell her he is quite all right,' I said. 'Tell her we are all safe. Tell her we love her. We are sorry she is all alone. Tell her to be brave and careful. No one must see that she is worried.'

Petra sent think-pictures to Rachel. Then she said :

'Rachel understands. She says she will try to be brave,' said Petra.

She thought for a moment. Then she said to me, in words :

'Rachel is afraid. She is crying inside. She wants Michael.'

'Did she tell you that?' I asked.

Petra shook her head. 'No. It was a sort of behind-think, but I saw it,' she said.

'We had better not say anything about it,' I said. 'It is nothing to do with us. We are not meant to see other people's behind-thinks. We must pretend you did not see it.'

'All right,' said Petra.

I hoped it was all right. I did not like the idea of seeing someone else's 'behind-thinks'. I was rather worried.

39 Waiting for Battle

Sophie woke up a few minutes later. She seemed calm now. She sent us to the back of the cave and took the skin off the front. Soon she lit a fire. Most of the smoke went outside the cave. Some stayed in the cave. But that would stop anyone seeing us.

Sophie put some food into an iron pot. She put some water in with it. Then she put the pot on the fire.

'Watch the pot,' she said to Rosalind. She went down the ladder.

After twenty minutes we saw her head at the top of the ladder. She threw some bread into the cave. Then she went to look at the pot.

'Is everything all right?' I asked her.

'Yes,' she said. 'They found the dead man. They think you did it. They went to look for you. But now they have other things to worry about. The men who went to the fighting are coming back in twos and threes. Do you know what happened?'

I told her how the Fringes men had tried to attack the Waknuk men. I told her that there had been too many Waknuk men and the Fringes men had run away.

'Where are the Waknuk men now?' asked Sophie.

I asked Michael.

'We have left the woods,' he said. 'We are coming into rough country now.'

I told Sophie what he had said.

'That means they will be at the river-bank in three hours,' she said.

She put the food into bowls. It was a sort of porridge. It did not taste too bad. But the bread was very hard. Petra said that it was not good food, like we had at home. That made her think of something. She said:

'Michael, is my father there?'

Her question surprised Michael. He said yes, without thinking. I looked at Petra. She did not understand what it meant. It meant my father was willing to kill Petra and me. I had thought my father might be with the Waknuk men. But it was still a shock to know that he was coming after us. I knew what his face would look like. He would look cold and angry. I thought about my poor Aunt Harriet. She had said: 'I will ask God to send love into the world.' How could there be love in the world when there was a man like my father in it?

Rosalind put her hands on my arms. Sophie looked up. She saw my face.

'What is the matter?' she asked.

Rosalind said: 'David's father is coming with the men from Waknuk. He wants to kill us. He will kill his own children.'

Sophie looked very shocked. I looked at her, then at Petra. I looked round the cave, and I looked at the rags Sophie wore.

I said: 'The Bible tells us to love our parents! Am I meant to forgive my father? Or am I meant to kill him?'

I did not know that I had sent a think-picture of that thought. Suddenly, the Zealand woman was talking.

'Leave your father alone,' she said. 'Your father, and men like him, will soon be dead. No one else will believe that they are right. We have a new world to win. They will only have to lose their wicked beliefs.'

Sophie was sitting by the front of the cave. She looked out. 'There are quite a lot of men back now,' she said. 'I think nearly all the Fringes men are back now. Some of them are standing by Gordon's tent. He must be back too.'

She finished her food. Then she said: 'I will see what I can find out.' She went quickly down the ladder.

She was gone for an hour. I looked out of the cave once or twice. I could see the spider-man in front of his tent. He was telling his Fringes men to get into groups. He was drawing plans on the earth.

Sophie came back at last.

'What is happening?' I asked her. 'What is the plan?'

She did not answer.

'For goodness sake,' I told her, 'we *want* the Fringes people to win. But we don't want Michael to get hurt. Tell me the plan!'

'We are going to wait until the men from Waknuk cross the river,' she said. 'Then we will attack them.'

I said to Michael: 'Try not to cross the river. Stay behind. Or pretend you have fallen off your horse. Then swim.'

'I will do that if I have to,' said Michael. 'But I will try to think of something else.'

A few moments later, a voice from outside the cave called: 'Sophie!' Sophie said quietly, 'It is Gordon. Keep back.' She ran across the cave and down the ladder.

After that nothing happened for more than an hour. Then the Zealand woman spoke again.

'Answer me, please, ' she said. 'We need to know exactly where you are. Just send number-pictures. Then I can tell how far away you are.'

Petra sent her strong think-pictures of numbers.

'All right,' the Zealand woman said. 'We will be with you quicker than we thought. Not more than a few hours now.'

Another half an hour went by. The camp looked almost empty now. There was no one near the huts and tents except a few women.

'We can see the river,' Michael said.

Twenty minutes went by. Then Michael said:

'The Fringes people have made a mistake, the fools. We saw two of them on top of the cliffs. Now we know their plan. We are going to stop to work things out.'

Ten minutes later, he said :

'This is our plan. We are going back and will stop right opposite the cliffs. We will go into some bushes. We will leave about six men outside the bushes. They will light fires and walk up and down. The Fringes people will think there are a lot of us there. But most of us will go down the river. We will cross the river from there. Tell Sophie all that if you can.'

The camp was not far behind the cliffs. I thought : if the Waknuk men come behind the cliffs this way we will be caught. I looked again at the camp. Perhaps we could run for it. There were still only a few women down in the camp. If we ran for it, would we run towards the Waknuk men and be caught by them? Then I saw that the women had got bows and arrows. I knew we would not be able to run for it now.

Michael had told me to tell Sophie about the Waknuk plan. But how could I tell her when she wasn't here? And even if I left Rosalind and Petra, I would never get to Sophie. The spider-man had given orders that I was to be shot if I came back to the camp. And anyone could see even from a long way away that I was not a Fringes man. Even if they did not know who I was they would shoot.

I wished that Sophie would come back.

'We have come across the river,' said Michael. 'We are very close. No Fringes men have tried to stop us.'

We went on waiting.

40   The Battle

Suddenly, a gun went off in the woods, on the left. There were three or more shots. Then silence. Then another two shots.

A few minutes later a lot of Fringes people came running out of the woods on the right. They ran to the left, where the guns had fired. There were both men and women, all dirty and wearing rags. You could see that some of them were Mutants, but a lot looked like dirty Norms. I could only see three or four guns being carried. Most of the Fringes people had bows and arrows. Some had short spears as well. I saw the spider-man, taller than any of them. Beside him was Sophie, with a bow and arrow in her hand.

'What is happening?' I asked Michael. 'Was that your lot shooting?'

'No,' he said. 'That was the other group. They want the Fringes men to run towards them. Then we will go after the Fringes people from behind.'

'That plan is working,' I said.

More guns went off on the left. There was a lot of shouting. A few arrows fell into the left of the clearing. Some Fringes men came running back out of the trees.

Suddenly there was a strong, clear think-picture.

'Are you still safe?' asked the Zealand woman.

We were all three lying on the floor of the cave by the opening. We could see what was happening. I did not think anyone would see us now.

Petra sent a sudden, strong think-picture, like a flash.

'Hold on, child! We are coming!' said the Zealand woman.

More arrows fell into the left-hand side of the clearing. More Fringes men came running into the clearing from the trees. They hid behind the huts and tents. Still more ran out. They were followed by a rain of arrows. The Fringes men stayed behind the huts. Sometimes they looked up and fired arrows quickly at the Waknuk men in the trees.

Then, suddenly, arrows flew into the clearing from the woods on the right. The Fringes people saw that they were trapped. Arrows were coming from right and left. They got very frightened. Most of them jumped to their feet. They started to run towards the cliffs. They were going to hide in the caves. I was ready to push away our ladder, to stop people climbing into our cave.

Then I saw six men on horses, riding out of the trees on the right. I saw the spider-man. He was standing by his tent. His bow was in his hand and he was watching the horsemen. Sophie was still beside him. She pulled at his shirt. She wanted him to run to the caves. He pushed her back with his long right arm, still looking at the horsemen. One of them was my father.

Suddenly the spider-man went stiff. He put up his bow like a flash, and pulled the string. He let his arrow fly. The arrow hit my father in the left side of his chest. He fell back on Sheba, my horse. Then he fell slowly to the ground.

The spider-man threw down his bow and turned. He picked up Sophie with his long arms and began to run. His long legs had only gone three strides when two arrows hit him in the back and side. He fell.

Sophie got up and ran on by herself. An arrow hit her in her right arm. She ran on, with the arrow still in her arm. Then another arrow hit her in the back of the neck. She fell to the ground, and her body slid along in the dust . . .

Petra had not seen that happen. She was looking all around.

'What is that queer noise?' she said.

The Zealand woman said calmly:

'Don't be frightened. We are coming. It is all right. Stay just where you are.'

I could hear the noise now. It was a strange noise, rather like drums. It got louder and louder. I could not tell where it was coming from.

More Waknuk men were coming out of the woods into the clearing, most of them on horses. I knew many of them. I had known them all my life. Now they were ready to kill us. Most of the Fringes people were now in the caves. They were shooting a little better now they were hidden.

Suddenly one of the horsemen shouted. He pointed to the sky.

41 The Flying-Ship

I looked up too. The sky was no longer clear. Something hung over us. It was like a bank of mist, but with quick bright flashes. Through the mist, I could see a strange, silver thing hanging in the sky above us.

It was the thing I had dreamt of when I was a child. I could not see it properly because of the mist. But it was just as I had dreamt it : silver and shining. Something was going round very fast on top of it. It got bigger and louder as it came down towards us.

I looked down again. A few, shining threads were falling slowly past the cave. Then more and more of them fell, catching the light as they came.

The shooting stopped. All over the clearing the Waknuk men put down their bows and guns and looked up. Then they shouted with fear and turned to run. Over on the right the horses started to run wild. In a few seconds, the whole place was full of shouting men and frightened horses. Men knocked each other over as they ran. Horses ran through the tents, kicking them down.

'Michael!' I called. 'Over here! Come this way.'

'I'm coming,' he told me.

I saw him then. He was getting to his feet beside a horse. The horse was on the ground, kicking strongly. Michael looked up towards our cave. He saw us and waved. He looked up again at the thing flying in the sky. It was still coming slowly down. It was only about two hundred feet above us now. Underneath it, the strange mist of threads moved.

'I'm coming,' said Michael again.

He turned towards us and started. Then he stopped. He tried to pull a thread off his arm. His hand stayed on his arm.

'That's funny,' he said. 'The thread is like a cobweb, but it is sticky. I can't move my hand . . .' Suddenly he sounded frightened. 'It is stuck. I can't move my hand!'

The Zealand woman spoke calmly:

'Don't try to move, Michael. You will get very tired. Lie down if you can. Keep calm. Just wait. Keep still, on the ground. Then the thread cannot get *round* you.'

I saw Michael do as she said, but I saw he was worried. Suddenly, I saw that over the clearing, men were trying to get the threads off themselves. But where their hands touched the threads, they got stuck. The men looked like flies in cobwebs. All the time, more and more threads were falling down on them. Most of the men tried to get the threads off and then tried to run to the trees, to hide. But they could not run properly. They ran a few steps and then their feet stuck together. They fell on the ground. They stuck to the threads on the ground. More threads fell on top of them. The men tried to move again, then gave up. They lay still. The same thing was happening to the horses. I saw one walk backwards into a bush. The bush swung round and touched the other leg. The legs stuck together. The horse fell over and lay kicking – for a while.

A thread fell on the back of my own hand. I told Rosalind and Petra to go right to the back of the cave. I looked at the thread on my hand. I tried to rub it off on the rock of the cave. I was not careful enough. As I moved, other threads moved towards me. My hand stuck to the rock.

'Here they are!' said Petra, in think-pictures and words together.

I looked up. The shining silver thing landed in the middle of the clearing. As it came down, a cloud of threads moved slowly upwards. I saw some of them move to the front of the cave. I shut my eyes. There was a light touch on my face.

When I tried to open my eyes, I could not.

42 Killer Threads

It is hard to lie still when you feel more and more sticky threads falling on you. They fell on my face and hands. Then they started to press on my skin and pull it.

I could hear Michael. He thought this was a trick. He thought he should have run away before. Before I could say anything, the Zealand woman said:

'It is all right. This is not a trick. Keep calm.'

'Have the threads got you too?' I asked Rosalind.

'Yes,' she said. 'The wind from the flying thing sent the threads right into the cave. Petra darling, you heard what the Zealand woman said. You must try to keep still.'

The loud noise of the flying-ship grew less. Soon it stopped. The silence was shocking. There were a few quiet moans, but little more. I knew why. The threads had fallen over my own mouth. I could not have called out.

We waited for a long time. My skin began to hurt with the pull of the threads.

The Zealand woman asked, 'Michael? Where are you? Keep counting, so that I can find you.'

Michael started counting, in number-pictures. When he got to twelve, I knew that he felt better. I heard him say in words:

'They are in that cave there, that one.'

I heard the ladder move. Then there was a hissing noise. Something wet fell on my face and hands. My skin stopped hurting. I slowly opened my eyes. My eyelids felt sticky.

Close in front of me, standing on the ladder, was a woman. She was quite hidden in a shiny white suit. There were still threads in the air, but when they fell on the suit they did not stick. The woman was wearing a strange helmet. I could only see eyes, looking at me through a little window in the helmet. The woman wore white gloves. She held a small bottle. Spray was hissing out of it.

'Turn over,' came the woman's think-picture.

I turned. The woman sprayed the front of my clothes. Then she climbed right into the cave. She stepped over me and went towards Rosalind and Petra at the back of the cave. She sprayed them too. Michael climbed up the ladder and into the cave. He, too, was wet with spray. I sat up and looked past him.

The silver flying-ship rested in the middle of the clearing. The thing on top of it had stopped spinning round. There were windows in the side of the flying-ship and a door was open.

The clearing looked as if thousands of spiders had made their cobwebs there. Threads were everywhere. They looked white now. I saw what made them different from cobwebs.

They did not move in the wind. And nothing else moved at all.

Men and horses lay near the tents. They were quite still.

There was a sudden sharp noise from the right. I looked over and saw a young tree break. It fell to the ground. Then I saw something else move. A bush slowly fell over. It pulled its roots up with it. Another bush fell. A hut fell down, and another. It was strange and frightening.

Back in the cave, Rosalind said: 'Thank goodness that is over.' I got up and went to her, with Michael following. Petra said:

'That was *very* horrid.'

She looked at the woman in the white suit. The woman sprayed all round the cave. Then she pulled off her gloves and lifted off her helmet. She looked at us and we looked back hard.

She had large brown-green eyes. Her eyelashes were long and golden. Her face was very pretty. Her hair was a bit darker than Rosalind's. We were surprised to see that her hair was short.

But what made us really look hard at her was the colour of her skin. It was perfect. It was pale cream and soft pink. It looked quite new. But the woman was not a young girl. She was about thirty. The woman looked at us very calmly. Then she looked hard at Petra. She smiled at Petra, showing perfect, white teeth.

As she looked at Petra, the Zealand woman's think-pictures were strange. She was happy and surprised at the same time. Petra could not really understand what the woman was thinking. But she looked at her in a special way. Petra knew that this was one of the most important times in her life.

Then, after a few moments, Petra smiled and laughed. We did not know what she and the Zealand woman were saying. But they were both very happy.

The Zealand woman bent down and picked Petra up.

They looked closely at each other's faces. Petra touched the woman's face. The Zealand woman laughed, and kissed Petra. Then she put her down again.

'It was worth coming,' she said. She spoke in words, but in a strange way. I could hardly understand what she said. 'It really was worth coming,' she said again.

Then she spoke in think-pictures again. It was much easier to understand her now.

'It was hard for us to get our Government to let us come,' she said. 'No one has ever been this far before. It cost so much to bring the flying ship. No one thought it was worth it. But it will be worth it . . .'

She shook her head again, as if she still could not believe Petra was so young, and could make such strong think-pictures. Then she said to me :

'Petra still has a lot to learn. But we will give her the best teachers. And one day she will be teaching them.'

She sat down on Sophie's bed of branches and skins. She looked at us all again. Then she nodded.

'You have been able to learn a lot too,' she said. 'But you will find there is a lot we can teach you.' She took Petra's hand. 'Well,' she said, 'as you have nothing to bring with you, we can go now.'

43 Michael and Rachel

Michael said, 'Are we going to Waknuk?'

'Why?' said the woman.

'Rachel is still there,' said Michael.

The Zealand woman thought about that.

'I'm not sure . . . wait a minute,' she told him.

She began to talk to someone on the flying-ship. They talked so fast that I could not understand what they were saying. Then she shook her head sadly.

'I am sorry,' she said, 'but we cannot go to get Rachel.'

'It would not take long. It isn't far, not for your flying-ship,' Michael said.

She shook her head again.

'I am sorry,' she said again. 'Of course we would get Rachel if we could. But, you see, the journey here was longer than we thought. Some of the places were so bad that we did not want to fly over them. We had to go round them. And we had to come very fast to get to you in time. The ship uses something called fuel. The further it goes, and the more people it carries, the more fuel is used. We have only enough fuel now to go straight to Zealand. If we went to Waknuk now and got Rachel, we would not have enough fuel to go back. We would fall in the sea and drown. Do you understand?' She stopped talking.

Suddenly we all felt the silence outside. Even the leaves on the trees did not move. Rosalind said:

'They are not — they are not all — *dead*? I didn't understand. I thought . . .'

'Yes,' said the Zealand woman. 'They are all dead. When the threads get dry they get very tight on the skin. If a man tries to get free, he soon blacks out. He dies quickly. It is kinder than your arrows and spears.'

Rosalind shivered. Perhaps I did, too. To fight with threads like that . . . it was quite different from a real battle. And the Zealand woman seemed so calm. She did not seem to care that everything outside was dead.

She saw what we were thinking and shook her head.

'It is not nice to kill anything,' she said. 'But you cannot live without killing things. You have to eat. And if other people want to kill you, you have to kill them.'

'The poor Fringes people had to live unhappily because

the people of Waknuk said they must. Now it is the turn of the Waknuk people to die. One day we will have to die. People will be born who are more important than us. We shall try to fight them, but we will not win. That is what life is about : it is about change. If you fight change, you are fighting life . . . If you still feel shocked, think about what the people of Waknuk wanted to do to you. They would have killed you . . .'

I found it hard to understand everything the Zealand woman said. But I thought about why we had to run away. I looked at Petra. I thought about my Aunt Harriet, drowned in the river, and I thought of poor Anne, who had hanged herself, and of Sally and Katherine and how they had been hurt. And I thought about Sophie, dying in the dust with an arrow in her neck . . .

Any of those things could have happened to Petra. I put my arm around her.

All the time the Zealand woman had been talking, Michael was looking out of the cave. He looked for a long time at the flying-ship in the clearing. Now he looked at the rock floor between his feet. Then he said :

'Petra, do you think you can talk to Rachel for me?'

Petra tried.

'Yes,' she said. 'She is there. She wants to know what is happening.'

'Tell her first that we are all alive. We are quite all right,' said Michael.

After a few moments Petra said : 'Yes, Rachel understands that.'

'Now I want you to tell her this,' said Michael carefully. 'Tell her that she must be very brave – and very careful. In a little time, perhaps three or four days, I will come and fetch her away. Will you tell her that?'

Petra sent all that message to Rachel. She waited for Rachel to answer. Then she made a small frown.

'Oh dear,' she said. 'Rachel is crying again. She does cry a lot, that girl, doesn't she? I don't see why. Her behind-thinks are not sad at all this time. It is sort of happy crying. Isn't that silly?'

We all looked at Michael. We did not say anything. But we wondered how he would go to fetch Rachel. In a way, we thought he should come with us.

Michael said: 'Rachel is quite *alone*. Would you leave Rosalind, David? Would Rosalind leave David?'

We did not answer.

'You said you would fetch her away,' said Rosalind.

'That is what I meant,' said Michael. 'We *could* stay in Waknuk for a time. We could wait until we were found out, or our children were found out . . . That's not good enough . . . Or we could come to the Fringes.'

He looked out across the clearing again.

'That is not good enough either. Rachel should have the best just as much as us. If the flying-ship can't take her, then someone must bring her.'

The Zealand woman was looking at him. She thought he was very brave, but she said:

'It is a very long way. And there are those black lands. You can't cross those.'

'I know that,' said Michael. 'But the world is round. I shall find another way.'

'But it will be very dangerous,' said the Zealand woman.

'It will be dangerous to stay in Waknuk. How can we stay there when we know that there is a place for people like us to go to? We have something to live for now.'

The Zealand woman thought for a moment. Then she looked at Michael again.

'When you do get to us, Michael,' she told him, 'you can be very sure of your place with us.'

44   The City in My Dream

The door of the flying-ship shut hard. The flying-ship started to shake and blow a great dusty wind across the clearing. Through the windows, we could see Michael, his clothes flapping in the wind.

The ground sloped below us. We rose faster and faster into the evening sky. Soon we were steady, pointing to the south-west.

Petra was very excited. Her think-pictures were very strong.

'It is so *exciting*!' she said. 'I can see for miles and miles and miles. Oh, Michael, you do look funny and small down there!' Michael waved. His thought came up to us:

'Just now,' he said, 'I *feel* very funny and small down here. But we shall come after you.'

The city was just like my dreams. The sun was very bright – much brighter than in Waknuk. It shone on bright blue sea in a bay and the sea was full of little boats. They had coloured sails. From the flying-ship I could see the houses round the bay and then the city in the hills. There were green parks and gardens. I could see tiny cars going along the roads. Inland, another flying-ship was going down to the city.

It was so like my dream that for a moment I thought I was back in my bed, in Waknuk. I took hold of Rosalind's hand.

'It *is* real, isn't it?' I said. 'You can see it too?'

'It is so pretty, David,' she said. 'And there is something else too. You didn't tell me about that.'

'What is it?' I asked.

'Listen! . . . Can't you feel it? Open your mind more . . .

Petra, darling, *please* stop sending such strong think-pictures. Just for a few minutes!'

I opened my mind. I could feel something like bees, buzzing. It was a mixture of buzzing and soft light.

'What is it?' I asked again.

'Don't you know, David? It is people. Lots and lots of our kind of people, sending think-pictures.'

I listened again, and I knew that she was right.

We had crossed the bay now. The city was very close.

'I am beginning to believe it is real and true at last,' I said to Rosalind.

She turned her head. The under-Rosalind was in her face. She was smiling. Her eyes shone. It was like a flower opening . . .

'This time, David . . .' she began. Then she suddenly stopped. We put our hands to our heads. Everyone cried out.

'Oh, sorry,' said Petra to all of us, and to the city. 'But it *is* very exciting.'

Rosalind laughed. 'This time, darling, we'll forgive you,' she said to Petra. 'It *is*.'